Marx
Abbott Hardy Machiavelli Cooper Emerson Joyce Austen
Defoe Montaigne Chesterton Hugo
Melville Haggard Eliot Grimm
Stoker Christie Carroll Molière
Wilde Maupassant Byron Schiller
Garnett Einstein Fitzgerald Engels Smith
Goethe Hawthorne Kafka
Cotton Dostoyevsky Hall
Baum Henry Kipling Doyle Willis
Leslie Dumas Nietzsche
Flaubert Turgenev Balzac
Stockton Vatsyayana Crane
Burroughs Verne
Curtis Tocqueville Gogol Vinci
Homer Widger Tolstoy Whitman Busch
Darwin Thoreau Twain
Potter Freud Zola Lawrence Scott
Kant Jowett Stevenson Dickens Plato Harte
Andersen Burton Hesse
London Descartes Cervantes
Poe Aristotle Wells Voltaire
Hale James Hastings Cooke
Bunner Shakespeare Irving
Richter Chambers da Vinci
Doré Dante Chekhov Ida Shaw Benedict Alcott
Swift Wodehouse Pushkin
Newton

ⓣ tredition®

tredition was established in 2006 by Sandra Latusseck and Soenke Schulz. Based in Hamburg, Germany, tredition offers publishing solutions to authors and publishing houses, combined with world-wide distribution of printed and digital book content. tredition is uniquely positioned to enable authors and publishing houses to create books on their own terms and without conventional manu-facturing risks.

For more information please visit: www.tredition.com

TREDITION CLASSICS

This book is part of the TREDITION CLASSICS series. The creators of this series are united by passion for literature and driven by the intention of making all public domain books available in printed format again - worldwide. Most TREDITION CLASSICS titles have been out of print and off the bookstore shelves for decades. At tredi-tion we believe that a great book never goes out of style and that its value is eternal. Several mostly non-profit literature projects pro-vide content to tredition. To support their good work, tredition donates a portion of the proceeds from each sold copy. As a reader of a TREDITION CLASSICS book, you support our mission to save many of the amazing works of world literature from oblivion. See all available books at www.tredition.com.

Project Gutenberg

The content for this book has been graciously provided by Project Gutenberg. Project Gutenberg is a non-profit organization founded by Michael Hart in 1971 at the University of Illinois. The mission of Project Gutenberg is simple: To encourage the creation and distribu-tion of eBooks. Project Gutenberg is the first and largest collection of public domain eBooks.

Early Plays —Catiline, the Warrior's Barrow, Olaf Liljekrans

Henrik Ibsen

Imprint

This book is part of TREDITION CLASSICS

Author: Henrik Ibsen
Cover design: Buchgut, Berlin – Germany

Publisher: tredition GmbH, Hamburg - Germany
ISBN: 978-3-8424-2940-6

www.tredition.com
www.tredition.de

The intention of the TREDITION CLASSICS series is to make world literature in the public domain available in printed format. Literary enthusiasts and organizations, such as Project Gutenberg, world-wide have scanned and digitally edited the original texts. tredition has subsequently formatted and redesigned the content into a modern reading layout. Therefore, we cannot guarantee the exact reproduction of the original format of a particular historic edition. Please also note that no modifications have been made to the spelling, therefore it may differ from the orthography used today.

SCANDINAVIAN CLASSICS

VOLUME XVII

EARLY PLAYS

by

HENRIK IBSEN

* * * * *

EARLY PLAYS

CATILINE, THE WARRIOR'S BARROW, OLAF LILJEKRANS

by

HENRIK IBSEN

TRANSLATED FROM THE NORWEGIAN
BY ANDERS ORBECK, A. M.

*Assistant Professor of English in the University
of Montana*

To

O. W. Firkins

Teacher and Friend
and Inspirer of these Translations._

CONTENTS

INTRODUCTION

One of the most remarkable facts about Ibsen is the orderly development of his genius. He himself repeatedly maintained that his dramas were not mere isolated accidents. In the foreword to the readers in the popular edition of 1898 he urges the public to read his dramas in the same order in which he had written them, deplores the fact that his earlier works are less known and less understood than his later works, and insists that his writings taken as a whole constitute an organic unity. The three of his plays offered here for the first time in English translation will afford those not familiar with the original Norwegian some light on the early stages of his development.

Catiline, the earliest of Ibsen's plays, was written in 1849, while Ibsen was an apothecary's apprentice in Grimstad. It appeared in Christiania in the following spring under the pseudonym Brynjolf Bjarme. The revolutionary atmosphere of 1848-49, the reading of the story of Catiline in Sallust and Cicero in preparation for the university examinations, the hostility which existed between the apprentice and his immediate social environment, the fate which the play met at the hands of the theatrical management and the publishers, his own struggles at the time, — are all set forth clearly enough in the preface to the second edition. The play was written in the blank verse of Oehlenschlaeger's romantic dramas. Ibsen's portrayal of the Roman politician is not in accord with tradition; Catiline is not an out-and-out reprobate, but an unfortunate and highly sensitive individual in whom idealism and licentiousness struggle for mastery. Vasenius, in his study of the poet (*Ibsens Dramatiska Diktning in dess Första Skede*, Helsingfors, 1879), insists that Ibsen thus intuitively hit upon the real Catiline revealed by later nineteenth century research. The poet seems not to have heard of Duma's *Catiline*, which appeared about the same time, nor of earlier plays on the subject by Ben Jonson and others. The struggle in Ibsen's play is

centered in the soul of Catiline; not once do his political oppo-
nents appear on the scene. Only one critic raised his voice in
behalf of the play at the time of its appearance, and only a few
copies of the original edition survive. Ibsen issued in 1875 a revised edition in celebration of his twenty-fifth anniversary as an
author. Since then a third edition has been issued in 1891, and a
fourth in 1913.

The Warrior's Barrow, Ibsen's second play, was finished in 1850
shortly after the publication of *Catiline*. Ibsen entered upon his
literary career with a gusto he seems soon to have lost; he wrote
to his friend Ole Schulerud in January, 1850, that he was work-
ing on a play about Olaf Trygvesson, an historical novel, and a
longer poem. He had begun *The Warrior's Barrow* while he was
still at Grimstad, but this early version, called *The Normans*, he
revised on reaching Christiania. In style and manner and even in
subject-matter the play echoes Oehlenschlaeger. Ibsen's vikings
are, however, of a fiercer type than Oehlenschlaeger's, and this
treatment of viking character was one of the things the critics,
bred to Oehlenschlaeger's romantic conception of more civilized
vikings, found fault with in Ibsen's play. The sketch fared better
than *Catiline*: it was thrice presented on the stage in Christiania
and was on the whole favorably reviewed. When Ibsen became
associated with the Bergen theater he undertook another revision of the play, and in this version the play was presented on
the stage in 1854 and 1856. The final version was published in
the *Bergenske Blad* in 1854, but no copy of this issue has survived;
the play remained inaccessible to the public until 1902, when it
was included in a supplementary volume (Volume X) to Ibsen's
collected works. The earlier version remained in manuscript
form until it was printed in 1917 in *Scandinavian Studies and
Notes* (Vol. IV, pp. 309-337).

Olaf Liljekrans, which was presented on the Bergen stage in
1857, marks the end of Ibsen's early romantic interest. The original idea for this play, which he had begun in 1850, he found in
the folk-tale "The Grouse in Justedal," about a girl who alone had
survived the Black Death in an isolated village. Ibsen had with

many others become interested in popular folk-tales and ballads. It was from Faye's *Norwegian Folk-Tales* (1844) that he took the story of "The Grouse in Justedal." His interest was so great that he even turned collector. Twice during this period he petitioned for and received small university grants to enable him to travel and "collect songs and legends still current among the people." Of the seventy or eighty "hitherto unpublished legends" which he collected on the first of these trips only a few have ever appeared in print; the results of his second trip are unknown. Ibsen had great faith in the availability of this medieval material for dramatic purposes; he even wrote an essay, "The Heroic Ballad and Its Significance for Artistic Poetry," urging its superior claims in contrast to that of the saga material, to which he was himself shortly to turn. The original play based on "The Grouse in Justedal" was left unfinished. After the completion of *Lady Inger of Östrât* and *The Feast at Solhoug* he came back to it, and taking a suggestion from the ballad in Landstad's collection (1852-3) he recast the whole play, substituted the ballad meter for the iambic pentameters, and called the new version *Olaf Liljekrans*. *Olaf Liljekrans* indicates clearly a decline in Ibsen's interest in pure romance. It is much more satirical than *The Feast at Solhoug*, and marks a step in the direction of those superb masterpieces of satire and romance, *Brand* and *Peer Gynt*. The play was twice presented on the stage in Bergen with considerable success, but the critics treated it harshly.

The relationship of the revised versions to the original versions of Ibsen's early plays is interesting, and might, if satisfactorily elucidated, throw considerable light on the development of his genius. It is evident that he was in this early period experimenting in metrical forms. He employed blank verse in *Catiline*, in the original version of *The Grouse in Justedal*, and even as late as 1853 in the revision of *The Warrior's Barrow*. There can be no question but that he was here following the Ochlenschlaeger tradition. Unrhymed pentameter, however, did not seem to satisfy him. He could with difficulty keep from falling into rhyme in *Catiline*, and in the early version of *The Warrior's Barrow* he used rhymed pentameters. After the revision of this play he threw aside blank verse altogether. "Iambic pentameter," he says in the essay on the heroic ballad, "is by no means the most suitable form for the treatment of ancient Scandinavian material; this form of verse is altogether foreign to our national meters, and it is surely through a national form that the national material can find its fullest expression." The folk-tale and the ballad gave him the suggestion he needed. In *The Feast at Solhoug* and the final version of *Olaf Liljekrans* he employed the ballad meter, and this form became the basis for the verse in all his later metrical plays.

Six years intervened between *The Grouse in Justedal* and *Olaf Liljekrans*, and the revision in this case amounted almost to the writing of a new play. Fredrik Paasche in his study (*Olaf Liljekrans*, Christiania, 1909) discusses the relation of *Olaf Liljekrans* to the earlier form of the play. Three years intervened between the first and final versions of *The Warrior's Barrow*. Professor A. M. Sturtevant maintains (*Journal of English and Germanic Philology*, XII, 407 ff.) that although "the influence of Ochlenschlaeger upon both versions of *The Warrior's Barrow* is unmistakable," yet "the two versions differ so widely from each other … that it may be assumed that … Ibsen had begun to free himself from the thraldom of Ochlenschlaeger's romantic conception of the viking character." He points out the influence of Welhaven and Heiberg on the second version, elaborates upon the superior character-delineation, and shows in considerable detail the "inner necessity … which brings about the change of heart in Gandalf and his warriors."

The revision of *Catiline* came twenty-five years after the original version, and consisted largely of linguistic changes. Ibsen seems never to have completely disowned this play; it has been included in all the complete editions, whereas *The Warrior's Barrow* and *Olaf Liljekrans* appear only in the first complete edition, and were even then relegated to a supplementary volume. In suggesting the revision of *Catiline*, Ibsen proposed "to make no change in the thought and ideas, but only in the language in which these are expressed; for the verses are, as Brandes has somewhere remarked, bad, — one reason being that the book was printed from my first rough uncorrected draft." He had at that time not developed his careful craftsmanship, and sought in the revision merely to put the drama into the form which he had originally had in mind, but which at that time he had been unable to achieve. The changes that were actually made are summarized by D. A. Seip (Ibsen, *Samlede Digter Verker*, 1918, VII, 114) who quotes Halvdan Koht and Julius Elias (Ibsen, *Efterladte Skrifter*, III): "The two editions 'agree in the sequence of tenses, with a few exceptions also in the sequence of speeches, and on the whole even in the sequence of lines. The changes involve principally the poetic expression itself; after the second act they become more and more extensive, and the last two acts have been augmented with 100 lines.' ... Not infrequently there appear words and expressions which are suggestive of Ibsen's later works."

These plays now appear for the first time in English translation. A. Johnstone published in *Translations from the Norse, by a B. S. S.* (Gloucester, about 1876), an English rendering of the first act of *Catiline* and a synopsis of the last two acts. William Archer explains at length his omission of *Catiline* from his edition of Ibsen. "A great part of the interest lies in the very crudities of its style, which it would be a thankless task to reproduce in translation. Moreover, the poet impaired even its biographical value by largely rewriting it before publication. He did not make it, or attempt to make it, a better play, but he in some measure corrected its juvenility of expression. Which version, then, should a translator choose? To go back to the original would seem a deliberate disregard of the poet's wishes; while, on the other hand, the retouched version is clearly of far inferior interest. It seems advisable, therefore, to leave the play alone, as far as this edition is concerned." *Olaf Liljekrans* and *The Warrior's Barrow* were acted in English in London in 1911 and 1912 respectively, but the English renderings used in these presentations have never appeared in print.

The text of *Catiline* in the present translation is that of the revised version as given in the edition of 1906-07; the text of the other two plays is that of the edition of 1898-1902. The meters of the original have been carefully reproduced. The great difficulty of rendering the ballad and lyrical meters of Ibsen into adequate English verse has made some stylistic changes necessary, such as the substitution of masculine for feminine rhymes, and the occasional alteration of the sense in slight measure.

I take this opportunity to acknowledge my gratitude to Professor O. W. Firkins, now of *The Weekly Review*, who suggested the translating of these plays and who offered from time to time invaluable criticisms; to Professor Howard M. Jones, of the University of Texas, Professor S. B. Hustvedt, of the University of Minnesota, and Professor W. W. Lawrence, of Columbia University, who read all or parts of these translations and made many helpful suggestions; and to Professor G. P. Krapp, of Columbia University, and my wife, who were of assistance in various ways.

ANDERS ORBECK.

New York, January 3, 1921.

* * * * *

CATILINE

A Drama in Three Acts

1850

* * * * *

PREFACE TO THE SECOND EDITION

The drama *Catiline*, with which I entered upon my literary career, was written during the winter of 1848-49, that is in my twenty-first year.

I was at the time in Grimstad, under the necessity of earning with my hands the wherewithal of life and the means for instruction preparatory to my taking the entrance examinations to the university. The age was one of great stress. The February revolution, the uprisings in Hungary and elsewhere, the Slesvig war, — all this had a great effect upon and hastened my development, however immature it may have remained for some time after. I wrote ringing poems of encouragement to the Magyars, urging them for the sake of liberty and humanity to hold out in the righteous struggle against the "tyrants"; I wrote a long series of sonnets to King Oscar, containing particularly, as far as I can remember, an appeal to set aside all petty considerations and to march forthwith at the head of his army to the aid of our brothers on the outermost borders of Slesvig. Inasmuch as I now, in contrast to those times, doubt that my winged appeals would in any material degree have helped the cause of the Magyars or the Scandinavians, I consider it fortunate that they remained within the more private sphere of the manuscript. I could

not, however, on more formal occasions keep from expressing myself in the impassioned spirit of my poetic effusions, which meanwhile brought me nothing—from friends or non-friends—but a
questionable reward; the former greeted me as peculiarly fitted for
the unintentionally droll, and the latter thought it in the highest
degree strange that a young person in my subordinate position
could undertake to inquire into affairs concerning which not even
they themselves dared to entertain an opinion. I owe it to truth to
add that my conduct at various times did not justify any great hope
that society might count on an increase in me of civic virtue, inasmuch as I also, with epigrams and caricatures, fell out with many
who had deserved better of me and whose friendship I in reality
prized. Altogether,—while a great struggle raged on the outside, I
found myself on a war-footing with the little society where I lived
cramped by conditions and circumstances of life.

Such was the situation when amid the preparations for my examinations I read through Sallust's *Catiline* together with Cicero's Cati-
linarian orations. I swallowed these documents, and a few months
later my drama was complete. As will be seen from my book, I did
not share at that time the conception of the two ancient Roman
writers respecting the character and conduct of Catiline, and I am
even now prone to believe that there must after all have been something great and consequential in a man whom Cicero, the assiduous
counsel of the majority, did not find it expedient to engage until
affairs had taken such a turn that there was no longer any danger
involved in the attack. It should also be remembered that there are
few individuals in history whose renown has been more completely
in the hands of enemies than that of Catiline.

My drama was written during the hours of the night. The leisure
hours for my study I practically had to steal from my employer, a
good and respectable man, occupied however heart and soul with
his business, and from those stolen study hours I again stole moments for writing verse. There was consequently scarcely anything
else to resort to but the night. I believe this is the unconscious reason that almost the entire action of the piece transpires at night.

Naturally a fact so incomprehensible to my associates as that I
busied myself with the writing of plays had to be kept secret; but a

twenty-year old poet can hardly continue thus without anybody being privy to it, and I confided therefore to two friends of my own age what I was secretly engaged upon.

The three of us pinned great expectations on *Catiline* when it had been completed. First and foremost it was now to be copied in order to be submitted under an assumed name to the theater in Christiania, and furthermore it was of course to be published. One of my faithful and trusting friends undertook to prepare a handsome and legible copy of my uncorrected draft, a task which he performed with such a degree of conscientiousness that he did not omit even a single one of the innumerable dashes which I in the heat of composition had liberally interspersed throughout wherever the exact phrase did not for the moment occur to me. The second of my friends, whose name I here mention since he is no longer among the living, Ole C. Schulerud, at that time a student, later a lawyer, went to Christiania with the transcript. I still remember one of his letters in which he informed me that *Catiline* had now been submitted to the theater; that it would soon be given a performance, — about that there could naturally be no doubt inasmuch as the management consisted of very discriminating men; and that there could be as little doubt that the booksellers of the town would one and all gladly pay a round fee for the first edition, the main point being, he thought, only to discover the one who would make the highest bid.

After a long and tense period of waiting there began to appear in the meantime a few difficulties. My friend had the piece returned from the management with a particularly polite but equally peremptory rejection. He now took the manuscript from bookseller to bookseller; but all to a man expressed themselves to the same effect as the theatrical management. The highest bidder demanded so and so much to publish the piece without any fee.

All this, however, was far from lessening my friend's belief in victory. He wrote to the contrary that it was best even so; I should come forward myself as the publisher of my drama; the necessary funds he would advance me; the profits we should divide in consideration of his undertaking the business end of the deal, except the proof-reading, which he regarded as superfluous in view of the handsome and legible manuscript the printers had to follow. In a later letter he declared that, considering these promising prospects for the future, he contemplated abandoning his studies in order to consecrate himself completely to the publishing of my works; two or three plays a year, he thought, I should with ease be able to write, and according to a calculation of probabilities he had made he had discovered that with our surplus we should at no distant time be able to undertake the journey so often agreed upon or discussed, through Europe and the Orient.

My journey was for the time being limited to Christiania. I arrived there in the beginning of the spring of 1850 and just previous to my arrival *Catiline* had appeared in the bookstalls. The drama created a stir and awakened considerable interest among the students, but the critics dwelt largely on the faulty verses and thought the book in other respects immature. A more appreciative judgment was uttered from but one single quarter, but this expression came from a man whose appreciation has always been dear to me and weighty and whom I herewith offer my renewed gratitude. Not very many copies of the limited edition were sold; my friend had a good share of them in his custody, and I remember that one evening when our domestic arrangements heaped up for us insurmountable difficulties, this pile of printed matter was fortunately disposed of as waste paper to a huckster. During the days immediately following we lacked none of the prime necessities of life.

During my sojourn at home last summer and particularly since my return here there loomed up before me more clearly and more sharply than ever before the kaleidoscopic scenes of my literary life. Among other things I also brought out *Catiline*. The contents of the book as regards details I had almost forgotten; but by reading it through anew I found that it nevertheless contained a great deal which I could still acknowledge, particularly if it be remembered that it is my first undertaking. Much, around which my later writings center, the contradiction between ability and desire, between will and possibility, the intermingled tragedy and comedy in humanity and in the individual, — appeared already here in vague foreshadowings, and I conceived therefore the plan of preparing a new edition, a kind of jubilee-edition, — a plan to which my publisher with his usual readiness gave his approval.

16

But it was naturally not enough simply to reprint without further ado the old original edition, for this is, as already pointed out, nothing but a copy of my imperfect and uncorrected concept or of the very first rough draft. In the rereading of it I remembered clearly what I originally had had in mind, and I saw moreover that the form practically nowhere gave a satisfactory rendering of what I had wished.

I determined therefore to revise this drama of my youth in a way in which I believe even at that time I should have been able to do it had the time been at my disposal and the circumstances more favorable for me. The ideas, the conceptions, and the development of the whole, I have not on the other hand altered. The book has remained the original; only now it appears in a complete form.

With this in mind I pray that my friends in Scandinavia and elsewhere will receive it; I pray that they will receive it as a greeting from me at the close of a period which to me has been full of changes and rich in contradictions. Much of what I twenty-five years ago dreamed has been realized, even though not in the manner nor as soon as I then hoped. Yet I believe now that it was best for me thus; I do not wish that any of that which lies between should have been untried, and if I look back upon what I have lived through I do so with thanks for everything and thanks to all.

HENRIK IBSEN.

Dresden, February, 1875.

* * * * *

DRAMATIS PERSONÆ

LUCIUS CATILINE A noble Roman.

AURELIA His wife.

FURIA A vestal.

CURIUS A youth related to Catiline.

MANLIUS An old warrior.

LENTULUS Young and noble Roman.

GABINIUS " " " "

STATILIUS " " " "

COEPARIUS " " " "

CETHEGUS " " " "

AMBIORIX Ambassador of the Allobroges.

OLLOVICO " " " "

An old MAN.

>PRIESTESSES and SERVANTS in the Temple of Vesta.

GLADIATORS and WARRIORS.

ESCORT of the Allobroges.

Sulla's GHOST.

* * * * *

SETTING

The first and second acts are laid in and near Rome, the third act in Etruria.

* * * * *

FIRST ACT

[The Flaminian Way outside of Rome. Off the road a wooded hillside. In the background loom the walls and the heights of the city. It is evening.]

[CATILINE stands on the hill among the bushes, leaning against a tree.]

CATILINE. I must! I must! A voice deep in my soul
Urges me on, — and I will heed its call.
Courage I have and strength for something better,
Something far nobler than this present life, —
A series of unbridled dissipations — !
No, no; they do not satisfy the yearning soul.

CATILINE. I rave and rave, — long only to forget.
'Tis past now, — all is past! Life has no aim.

CATILINE. [After a pause.]
And what became of all my youthful dreams?
Like flitting summer clouds they disappeared,
Left naught behind but sorrow and remorse; —
Each daring hope in turn fate robbed me of.

[He strikes his forehead.]

CATILINE. Despise yourself! Catiline, scorn yourself!
You feel exalted powers in your soul; —
And yet what is the goal of all your struggle?
The surfeiting of sensual desires.

CATILINE. [More calmly.]
But there are times, such as the present hour,
When secret longings kindle in my breast.

Ah, when I gaze on yonder city, Rome,
The proud, the rich, — and when I see that ruin
And wretchedness to which it now is sunk
Loom up before me like the flaming sun, —
Then loudly calls a voice within my soul:
Up, Catiline; — awake and be a man!

CATILINE. [Abruptly.] Ah, these are but delusions of the night,
Mere dreaming phantoms born of solitude.
At the slightest sound from grim reality, —
They flee into the silent depths within.

[The ambassadors of the Allobroges, AMBIORIX and OLLOVI-
CO, with their Escort, come down the highway without noticing
CATILINE.]

AMBIORIX. Behold our journey's end! The walls of Rome!
To heaven aspires the lofty Capitol.

OLLOVICO. So that is Rome? Italy's overlord,
Germany's soon, — and Gaul's as well, perchance.

AMBIORIX. Ah, yes, alas; — so it may prove betimes;
The sovereign power of Rome is merciless;
It crushes all it conquers, down to earth.
Now shall we see what lot we may expect:
If here be help against the wrongs at home,
And peace and justice for our native land.

OLLOVICO. It will be granted us.

AMBIORIX. So let us hope;
For we know nothing yet with certainty.

OLLOVICO. You fear somewhat, it seems?

AMBIORIX. And with good reason.
Jealous was ever Rome of her great power.
And bear in mind, this proud and haughty realm
Is not by chieftains ruled, as is our land.
At home the wise man or the warrior reigns, —
The first in wisdom and in war the foremost;
Him choose we as the leader of our people,
As arbiter and ruler of our tribe.
But here —

CATILINE. [Calls down to them.]
— Here might and selfishness hold sway; —
Intrigue and craft are here the keys to power.

　OLLOVICO. Woe to us, brethren, woe! He spies upon us.

AMBIORIX. [To CATILINE.]
Is such the practice of the high-born Roman?
A woman's trick we hold it in our nation.

CATILINE. [comes down on the road.]
Ah, have no fear; — spying is not my business;
By chance it was I heard your conversation. —
Come you from Allobrogia far away?
Justice you think to find in Rome? Ah, never!
Turn home again! Here tyranny holds sway,
And rank injustice lords it more than ever.
Republic to be sure it is in name;
And yet all men are slaves who cringe and cower,
Vassals involved in debt, who must acclaim
A venal senate — ruled by greed and power.
Gone is the social consciousness of old,
The magnanimity of former ages; —
Security and life are favors sold,
Which must be bargained for with hire and wages.
Not righteousness, but power here holds sway;
The noble man is lost among the gilded —

21

AMBIORIX. But say, — who then are you to tear away
The pillars of the hope on which we builded?

CATILINE. A man who burns in freedom's holy zeal;
An enemy of all unrighteous power;
Friend of the helpless trodden under heel, —
Eager to hurl the mighty from their tower.

AMBIORIX. The noble race of Rome — ? Ah, Roman, speak —
Since we are strangers here you would deceive us?
Is Rome no more the guardian of the weak,
The dread of tyrants, — ready to relieve us?

CATILINE. [Points towards the city and speaks.]
Behold the mighty Capitol that towers
On yonder heights in haughty majesty.
See, in the glow of evening how it lowers,
Tinged with the last rays of the western sky. —
So too Rome's evening glow is fast declining,
Her freedom now is thraldom, dark as night. —
Yet in her sky a sun will soon be shining,
Before which darkness quick will take its flight.

   [He goes.]

   * * * * *

   [A colonnade in Rome.]

   [LENTULUS, STATILIUS, COEPARIUS, and CETHEGUS enter,
in eager conversation.]

COEPARIUS. Yes, you are right; things go from bad to worse;
And what the end will be I do not know.

CETHEGUS. Bah! I am not concerned about the end.
The fleeting moment I enjoy; each cup
Of pleasure as it comes I empty, — letting

All else go on to ruin as it will.

LENTULUS. Happy is he who can. I am not blessed
With your indifference, that can outface
The day when nothing shall be left us more,
Nothing with which to pay the final score.

STATILIUS. And not the faintest glimpse of better things!
Yet it is true: a mode of life like ours —

CETHEGUS. Enough of that!

LENTULUS. Today because of debt
The last of my inheritance was seized.

CETHEGUS. Enough of sorrow and complaint! Come, friends!
We'll drown them in a merry drinking bout!

COEPARIUS. Yes, let us drink. Come, come, my merry comrades!

LENTULUS. A moment, friends; I see old Manlius yonder, —
Seeking us out, I think, as is his wont.

MANLIUS. [Enters impetuously.]
Confound the shabby dogs, the paltry scoundrels!
Justice and fairness they no longer know!

LENTULUS. Come, what has happened? Wherefore so embittered?

STATILIUS. Have usurers been plaguing you as well?

MANLIUS. Something quite different. As you all know,
I served with honor among Sulla's troops;
A bit of meadow land was my reward.
And when the war was at an end, I lived
Thereon; it furnished me my daily bread.
Now is it taken from me! Laws decree —

State property shall to the state revert
For equal distribution. Theft, I say, —
It is rank robbery and nothing else!
Their greed is all they seek to satisfy.

COEPARIUS. Thus with our rights they sport to please themselves.
The mighty always dare do what they will.

CETHEGUS. [Gaily.] Hard luck for Manlius! Yet, a worse mishap
Has come to me, as I shall now relate.
Listen, — you know my pretty mistress, Livia, —
The little wretch has broken faith with me,
Just now when I had squandered for her sake
The slender wealth that still remained to me.

STATILIUS. Extravagance — the cause of your undoing.

CETHEGUS. Well, as you please; but I will not forego
My own desires; these, while the day is fair,
To their full measure I will satisfy.

MANLIUS. And I who fought so bravely for the glory
And might which now the vaunting tyrants boast!
I shall —! If but the brave old band were here,
My comrades of the battlefield! But no;
The greater part of them, alas, is dead;
The rest live scattering in many lands. —

MANLIUS. Oh, what are you, the younger blood, to them?
You bend and cringe before authority;
You dare not break the chains that bind you fast;
You suffer patiently this life of bondage!

LENTULUS. By all the Gods, — although indeed he taunts us,
Yet, Romans, is there truth in what he says.

24

CETHEGUS. Oh, well,—what of it? He is right, we grant,
But where shall we begin? Ay, there's the rub.

LENTULUS. Yes, it is true. Too long have we endured
This great oppression. Now—now is the time
To break the bonds asunder that injustice
And vain ambition have about us forged.

STATILIUS. Ah, Lentulus, I understand. Yet hold;
For such a thing we need a mighty leader,—
With pluck and vision. Where can he be found?

LENTULUS. I know a man who has the power to lead us.

MANLIUS. Ah, you mean Catiline?

LENTULUS. The very man.

CETHEGUS. Yes, Catiline perchance is just the man.

MANLIUS. I know him well. I was his father's friend;
Many a battle side by side we fought.
Often his young son went with him to war.
Even his early years were wild and headstrong;
Yet he gave open proof of rare endowments,—
His mind was noble, dauntless was his courage.

LENTULUS. We'll find him, as I think, most prompt and willing.
I met him late this evening much depressed;
He meditates in secret some bold plan;—
Some desperate scheme he long has had in mind.

STATILIUS. No doubt; the consulate he long has sought.

LENTULUS. His efforts are in vain; his enemies
Have madly raged against him in the senate;—
He was himself among them; full of wrath
He left the council—brooding on revenge.

STATILIUS. Then will he surely welcome our proposal.

LENTULUS. I hope so. Yet must we in secret weigh
Our enterprise. The time is opportune.

[They go.]

* * * * *

[In the Temple of Vesta in Rome. On an altar in the background
burns a lamp with the sacred fire.]

[CATILINE, followed by CURIUS, comes stealing in between the
pillars.]

CURIUS. What, Catiline, — you mean to bring me here?
In Vesta's temple!

CATILINE. [Laughing.] Well, yes; so you see!

CURIUS. Ye gods, — what folly! On this very day
Has Cicero denounced you in the council;
And yet you dare —

CATILINE. Oh, let that be forgotten!

CURIUS. You are in danger, and forget it thus —
By rushing blindly into some new peril.

CATILINE. [Gaily.] Well, change is my delight. I never knew
Ere now a vestal's love, — forbidden fruit; —
Wherefore I came to try my fortune here.

CURIUS. What, — here, you say? Impossible! A jest!

CATILINE. A jest? Why, yes, — as all my loving is.
And yet I was in earnest when I spoke.
During the recent games I chanced to see
The priestesses in long and pompous train.
By accident I cast my roving eye
On one of them, — and with a hasty glance

She met my gaze. It pierced me to the soul.
Ah, the expression in those midnight eyes
I never saw before in any woman.

    CURIUS. Yes, yes, I know. But speak — what followed then?

CATILINE. A way into the temple I have found,
And more than once I've seen and spoken to her.
Oh, what a difference between this woman
And my Aurelia!

CURIUS. And you love them both
At once? No, — that I cannot understand.

CATILINE. Yes, strange, indeed; I scarcely understand myself.
And yet — I love them both, as you have said.
But oh, how vastly different is this love!
The one is kind: Aurelia often lulls
With soothing words my soul to peace and rest; —
But Furia —. Come, away; some one approaches.

    [They hide themselves among the pillars.]

FURIA. [Enters from the opposite side.]
Oh, hated walls, — witnesses of my anguish.
Home of the torment I must suffer still!
My hopes and cherished aspirations languish
Within my bosom, — now with feverish chill
Pervaded, now with all the heat of passion,
More hot and burning than yon vestal fire.

FURIA. Ah, what a fate! And what was my transgression
That chained me to this temple-prison dire, —
That robbed my life of every youthful pleasure, —
In life's warm spring each innocent delight?

FURIA. Yet tears I shall not shed in undue measure;
Hatred and vengeance shall my heart excite.

CATILINE. [Comes forward.]
Not even for me, my Furia, do you cherish
Another feeling, — one more mild than this?

FURIA. Ye gods! you, reckless man, — you here again?
Do you not fear to come — ?

CATILINE. I know no fear.
'Twas always my delight to mock at danger.

FURIA. Oh, splendid! Such is also my delight; —
This peaceful temple here I hate the more,
Because I live in everlasting calm,
And danger never lurks within its walls.

FURIA. Oh, this monotonous, inactive life,
A life faint as the flicker of the lamp — !
How cramped a field it is for all my sum
Of fervid longings and far-reaching plans!
Oh, to be crushed between these narrow walls; —
Life here grows stagnant; every hope is quenched;
The day creeps slowly on in drowsiness, —
And not one single thought is turned to deeds.

CATILINE. O Furia, strange, in truth, is your complaint!
It seems an echo out of my own soul, —
As if with flaming script you sought to paint
My every longing towards a worthy goal.
Rancour and hate in my soul likewise flourish;
My heart — as yours — hate tempers into steel;
I too was robbed of hopes I used to nourish;
An aim in life I now no longer feel.

CATILINE. In silence still I mask my grief, my want;
And none can guess what smoulders in my breast.
They scoff and sneer at me, — these paltry things;
They can not grasp how high my bosom beats
For right and freedom, all the noble thoughts
That ever stirred within a Roman mind.

FURIA. I knew it! Ah, your soul, and yours alone,
Is born for me, — thus clearly speaks a voice
That never fails and never plays me false.
Then come! Oh, come — and let us heed the call.

    CATILINE. What do you mean, my sweet enthusiast?

FURIA. Come, — let us leave this place, flee far away,
And seek a new and better fatherland.
Here is the spirit's lofty pride repressed;
Here baseness smothers each auspicious spark
Ere it can break into a burning flame.
Come, let us fly; — lo, to the free-born mind
The world's wide compass is a fatherland!

    CATILINE. Oh, irresistibly you lure me on —

FURIA. Come, let us use the present moment then!
High o'er the hills, beyond the sea's expanse, —
Far, far from Rome we first will stay our journey.
Thousands of friends will follow you outright;
In foreign lands we shall a home design;
There shall we rule; 'twill there be brought to light
That no hearts ever beat as yours and mine.

CATILINE. Oh, wonderful! — But flee? Why must we flee?
Here too our love for freedom can be nourished;
Here also is a field for thought and action,
As vast as any that your soul desires.

FURIA. Here, do you say? Here, in this paltry Rome,
Where naught exists but thraldom and oppression?
Ah, Lucius, are you likewise one of those
Who can Rome's past recall without confession
Of shame? Who ruled here then? Who rule to-day?
Then an heroic race—and now a rabble,
The slaves of other slaves—

CATILINE. Mock me you may;—
Yet know,—to save Rome's freedom from this babble,
To see yet once again her vanished splendor,
Gladly I should, like Curtius, throw myself
Into the abyss—

FURIA. I trust you, you alone;
Your eyes glow bright; I know you speak the truth.
Yet go; the priestesses will soon appear;
Their wont it is to meet here at this hour.

CATILINE. I go; but only to return again.
A magic power binds me to your side;—
So proud a woman have I never seen.

FURIA. [With a wild smile.] Then pledge me this; and swear that
you will keep Whatever you may promise. Will you, Lucius?

CATILINE. I will do aught my Furia may require;
Command me,—tell me what am I to promise.

FURIA. Then listen. Though I dwell a captive here,
I know there lives a man somewhere in Rome
Whom I have sworn deep enmity to death—
And hatred even beyond the gloomy grave.

CATILINE. And then—?

FURIA. Then swear, my enemy shall be
Your enemy till death. Will you, my Lucius?

CATILINE. I swear it here by all the mighty gods!
I swear it by my father's honored name
And by my mother's memory —! But, Furia, —
What troubles you? Your eyes are wildly flaming, —
And white as marble, deathlike, are your cheeks.

FURIA. I do not know myself. A fiery stream
Flows through my veins. Swear to the end your oath!

CATILINE. Oh, mighty powers, pour out upon this head
Your boundless fury, let your lightning wrath
Annihilate me, if I break my oath;
Aye, like a demon I shall follow him!

FURIA. Enough! I trust you. Ah, my heart is eased.
In your hand now indeed rests my revenge.

CATILINE. It shall be carried out. But tell me this, —
Who is your foe? And what was his transgression?

FURIA. Close by the Tiber, far from the city's tumult,
My cradle stood; it was a quiet home!
A sister much beloved lived with me there,
A chosen vestal from her childhood days. —
Then came a coward to our distant valley; —
He saw the fair, young priestess of the future —

   CATILINE. [Surprised.] A priestess? Tell me —! Speak —!

FURIA. He ravished her.
She sought a grave beneath the Tiber's stream.

CATILINE. [Uneasy.] You know him?

FURIA. I have never seen the man.
When first I heard the tidings, all was past.
His name is all I know.

CATILINE. Then speak it out!

FURIA. Now is it famed. His name is Catiline.

CATILINE. [Taken aback.]
What do you say? Oh, horrors! Furia, speak—!

FURIA. Calm yourself! What perturbs you? You grow pale.
My Lucius,—is this man perhaps your friend?

CATILINE. My friend? Ah, Furia, no;—no longer now.
For I have cursed,—and sworn eternal hate
Against myself.

FURIA. You—you are Catiline?

CATILINE. Yes, I am he.

FURIA. My Sylvia you disgraced?
Nemesis then indeed has heard my prayer;—
Vengeance you have invoked on your own head!
Woe on you, man of violence! Woe!

CATILINE. How blank
The stare is in your eye. Like Sylvia's shade
You seem to me in this dim candle light.

[He rushes out; the lamp with the sacred fire goes out.]

FURIA. [After a pause.] Yes, now I understand it. From my eyes
The veil is fallen,—in the dark I see.
Hatred it was that settled in my breast,
When first I spied him in the market-place.

A strange emotion; like a crimson flame!
Ah, he shall know what such a hate as mine,
Constantly brewing, never satisfied,
Can fashion out in ruin and revenge!

A VESTAL. [Enters.] Go, Furia, go; your watch is at an end;
Therefore I came —. Yet, sacred goddess, here —
Woe unto you! The vestal fire is dead!

FURIA. [Bewildered.]
Dead, did you say? So bright it never burned; —
'Twill never, never die!

   THE VESTAL. Great heavens, — what is this?

FURIA. The fires of hate are not thus lightly quenched!
Behold, love bursts forth of a sudden, — dies
Within the hour; but hate —

THE VESTAL. By all the gods, —
This is sheer madness!

   [Calls out.]

   THE VESTAL. Come! Oh, help! Come, help!

   [VESTALS and temple SERVANTS rush in.]

   SOME. What is amiss?

   OTHERS. The vestal fire is dead!

   FURIA. But hate burns on; revenge still blazes high!

   THE VESTALS. Away with her to trial and punishment!

   [They carry her out between them.]

CURIUS. [Comes forward.]
To prison now they take her. Thence to death. —
No, no, by all the gods, this shall not be!

Must she, most glorious of womankind,
Thus perish in disgrace, entombed alive? —
Oh, never have I felt so strangely moved.
Is this then love? Yes, love it is indeed. —
Then shall I set her free! — But Catiline?
With hate and vengeance will she follow him.
Has he maligners not enough already?
Dare I still others to their number add?
He was to me as were an elder brother;
And gratitude now bids me that I shield him. —
But what of love? Ah, what does it command?
And should he quake, the fearless Catiline,
Before the intrigues of a woman? No; —
Then to the rescue work this very hour!
Wait, Furia; — I shall drag you from your grave
To life again, — though at the risk of death!

   [He goes away quickly.]

   * * * * *

   [A room in CATILINE's house.]

CATILINE. [Enters impetuous and uneasy.]
"Nemesis then indeed has heard my prayer,
Vengeance you have invoked on your own head!"
Such were the words from the enchantress' lips.
Remarkable! Perchance it was a sign, —
A warning of what time will bring to me.

CATILINE. Now therefore I have pledged myself on oath
The blood avenger of my own misdeed.
Ah, Furia, — still I seem to see your eye,
Wildly aflame like that of death's own goddess!
Your words still echo hollow in my ears; —
The oath I shall remember all my life.

   [During the following AURELIA enters and approaches him unnoticed.]

34

CATILINE. Yet, it is folly now to go on brooding
Upon this nonsense; it is nothing else.
Far better things there are to think upon;
A greater work awaits my energies.
The restless age is urgent with its plea;
Toward this I must direct my thought in season;
Of hope and doubt I am a stormy sea —

AURELIA. [Seizes his hand.]
And may not your Aurelia know the reason?
May she not know what moves within your breast,
What stirs therein and rages with such madness?
May she not cheer and soothe your soul to rest,
And banish from your brow its cloud of sadness?

CATILINE. [Tenderly.] O, my Aurelia, — O, how kind and tender —.
Yet why should I embitter all your life?
Why should I share with you my many sorrows?
For my sake you have borne enough of anguish.
Henceforth upon my own head I shall bear
What ill-designing fate allotted me, —
The curse that lies in such a soul as mine,
Full of great spiritual energies,
Of fervent longings for a life of deeds,
Yet dwarfed in all its work by sordid cares. —
Must you, too, sharing in my wretched life,
Bitter with blasted hopes, then with me perish?

AURELIA. To comfort is the role of every wife,
Though dreams of greatness she may never cherish.
When the man, struggling for his lofty dream,
Reaps nothing but adversity and sorrow, —
Her words to him then sweet and tender seem,
And give him strength sufficient for the morrow;
And then he sees that even the quiet life
Has pleasures which the most tumultuous lacks.

CATILINE. Yes, you are right; I know it all too well.
And yet I cannot tear myself away.
A ceaseless yearning surges in my breast, —
Which only life's great tumult now can quiet.

AURELIA. Though your Aurelia be not all to you, —
Though she can never still your restless soul, —
Your heart yet open to a gentle word,
A word of comfort from your loving wife.
Though she may never slake your fiery thirst,
Nor follow in their flight your noble thoughts, —
Know this, that she can share your every sorrow,
Has strength and fortitude to ease your burden.

CATILINE. Then listen, dear Aurelia; you shall hear
What has of late depressed so deep my spirits.
You know, I long have sought the consulate —
Without avail. You know the whole affair —
How to increase the votes for my election,
I have expended —

AURELIA. Catiline, no more;
You torture me —

CATILINE. Do you too blame my course?
What better means therefor had I to choose? —
In vain I lavished all that I possessed;
My one reward was mockery and shame.
Now in the senate has my adversary,
The crafty Cicero, trampled me to earth.
His speech was a portrayal of my life,
So glaring that I, even I, must gasp.
In every look I read dismay and fear;
With loathing people speak of Catiline;
To races yet unborn my name will be
A symbol of a low and dreadful union
Of sensuality and wretchedness,

Of scorn and ridicule for what is noble.—
And there will be no deed to purge this name
And crush to earth the lies that have been told!
Each will believe whatever rumor tells—

AURELIA. But I, dear husband, trust no such reports.
Let the whole world condemn you if it will;
And let it heap disgrace upon your head;—
I know you hide within your inmost soul
A seed that still can blossom and bear fruit.
Only it cannot burst forth here in Rome;
Poisonous weeds would quickly prove the stronger.
Let us forsake this degradation's home;—
What binds you here? Why should we dwell here longer?

CATILINE. I should forsake the field,—and go away?
I should my greatest dreams in life surrender?
The drowning man still clutches firm and fast
The broken spars—though hope is frail and slender;
And should the wreck be swallowed in the deep,
And the last hope of rescue fail forever,—
Still clings he to the lone remaining spar,
And sinks with it in one last vain endeavor.

AURELIA. But should a kindly seacoast smile on him,
With groves all green along the rolling billows,
Hope then awakens in his heart again,—
He struggles inward, toward the silvery willows.
There reigns a quiet peace; 'tis beautiful;
There roll the waves, in silence, without number;
His heated brow sweet evening breezes cool,
As weary-limbed he rests himself in slumber;
Each sorrow-laden cloud they drive away;
A restful calm his weary mind assuages;—
There he finds shelter and prolongs his stay
And soon forgets the sorry by-gone ages.
The distant echo of the world's unrest

Alone can reach his dwelling unfrequented.
It does not break the calm within his breast; —
It makes his soul more happy and contented;
It calls to mind the by-gone time of strife,
Its shattered hopes and its unbridled pleasures;
He finds twice beautiful this quiet life —
And would not change it for the greatest treasures.

CATILINE. You speak the truth; and in this very hour
From strife and tumult I could go with you.
But can you name me some such quiet spot,
Where we can live in shelter and in peace?

AURELIA. [Joyful.] You will go, Catiline? What happiness, —
Oh, richer than my bosom can contain!
Let it be so, then! Come! This very night
We'll go away —

CATILINE. But whither shall we go?
Name me the spot where I may dare to rest
My head in homely peace!

AURELIA. How can you ask?
Have you forgot our villa in the country,
Wherein I passed my childhood days, where since,
Enraptured during love's first happy dawn,
We two spent many a blithesome summer day?
Where was the grass indeed so green as there?
Where else the groves so shady and sweet-smelling?
The snow-white villa from its wooded lair
Peeps forth and bids us there to make our dwelling.
There let us flee and dedicate our life
To rural duties and to sweet contentment; —
You will find comfort in a loving wife,
And through her kisses banish all resentment.

[Smiling.]

AURELIA. And when with all the flowers of the land
You come to me, your sovereign, in my bowers,
Then shall I crown you with the laurel band,
And cry, All hail to you, my king of flowers! —
But why do you grow pale? Wildly you press
My hand, — and strangely now your eyes are glowing —

CATILINE. Aurelia, alas, past is your happiness; —
There we can never, never think of going.
There we can never go!

AURELIA. You frighten me!
Yet, surely, — you are jesting, Catiline?

CATILINE. I jest! Would only that it were a jest!
Each word you speak, like the avenging dart
Of Nemesis, pierces my heavy heart,
Which fate will never grant a moment's rest.

AURELIA. O gods! speak, speak! What do you mean?

CATILINE. See here!
Here is your villa, — here your future joys!

[He draws out a purse filled with gold and throws it on the table.]

AURELIA. Oh, you have sold — ?

CATILINE. Yes, — all I sold today; —
And to what end? In order to corrupt —

AURELIA. O Catiline, no more! Let us not think
On this affair; sorrow is all it brings.

CATILINE. Your quiet-patience wounds me tenfold more
Than would a cry of anguish from your lips!

[An old SOLDIER enters and approaches CATILINE.]

THE SOLDIER. Forgive me, master, that thus unannounced
I enter your abode at this late hour.
Ah, be not wroth—

CATILINE. What is your errand here?

THE SOLDIER. My errand here is but a humble prayer,
Which you will hear. I am a needy man,
One who has sacrificed his strength for Rome.
Now I am feeble, can no longer serve;
Unused my weapons rust away at home.
The hope of my old age was in a son,
Who labored hard and was my one support.
Alas,—in prison now he's held for debt.
And not a ray of hope—. Oh, help me, master!

[Kneeling.]

THE SOLDIER. If but a penny! I have gone on foot
From house to house; each door is long since closed.
I know not what to do—

CATILINE. The paltry knaves!
A picture this is of the many's want.
Thus they reward the old brave company.
No longer gratitude is found in Rome!
Time was I might have wished in righteous wrath
To punish them with sword and crimson flames;
But tender words have just been spoken here;
My soul is moved; I do not wish to punish;—
To ease misfortune likewise is a deed.—
Take this, old warrior;—clear with this your debt.

[He hands him the purse with the gold.]

THE SOLDIER. [Rising.]
O gracious lord, — dare I believe your words?

CATILINE. Yes; but be quick, old man; go free your son.

[The SOLDIER goes hurriedly out.]

CATILINE. A better use, — not so, Aurelia dear? —
Than bribery and purchasing of votes?
Noble it is to crush the tyrant's might;
Yet quiet solace too has its reward.

AURELIA. [Throws herself in his arms.]
Oh, rich and noble is your spirit still.
Yes, — now I know my Catiline again.

* * * * *

[An underground tomb with a freshly walled-in passage high on the rear wall. A lamp burns faintly.]

[FURIA, in long black robes, is standing in the tomb as if listening.]

FURIA. A hollow sound. 'Tis thunder rolls above.
I hear its rumble even in the tomb.
Yet is the tomb itself so still — so still!
Am I forever damned to drowsy rest?
Never again am I to wander forth
By winding paths, as ever was my wish?

FURIA. [After a pause.]
A strange, strange life it was; — as strange a fate.
Meteor-like all came — and disappeared.
He met me. A mysterious magic force,
An inner harmony, together drew us.
I was his Nemesis; — and he my victim; —

Yet punishment soon followed the avenger.

FURIA. [Another pause.]
Now daylight rules the earth. — Am I perchance
To slip — unknowing — from the realm of light?
'Tis well, if so it be, — if this delay
Within the tomb be nothing but a flight
Upon the wings of lightning into Hades, —
If I be nearing even now the Styx!
There roll the leaden billows on the shore;
There silently old Charon plies his boat.
Soon am I there! Then shall I seat myself
Beside the ferry, — question every spirit,
Each fleeting shadow from the land of life,
As light of foot he nears the river of death, —
Shall ask each one in turn how Catiline
Fares now among the mortals of the earth, —
Shall ask each one how he has kept his oath.
I shall illumine with blue sulphur light
Each spectral countenance and hollow eye, —
To ascertain if it be Catiline.
And when he comes, then shall I follow him; —
Together we shall make the journey hence,
Together enter Pluto's silent hall.
I too a shadow shall his shade pursue; —
Where Catiline is, must Furia also be!

FURIA. [After a pause, more faintly.]
The air is growing close and clammy here, —
And every breath in turn more difficult. —
Thus am I drawing near the gloomy swamps,
Where creep the rivers of the underworld.

FURIA. [She listens; a dull noise is heard.]
A muffled sound? 'Tis like the stroke of oars.
It is the ferryman of shades who comes

To take me hence. No, here—here will I wait!

[The stones in the freshly walled-in passage are broken asunder.
CURIUS comes into view on the outside; he beckons to her.]

FURIA. Ah, greetings, Charon! Are you ready now
To lead me hence, a guest among the spirits?
Here will I wait!

    CURIUS. [Whispering.] I come to set you free!

    * * * * *

SECOND ACT

[A room in CATILINE's house with a colonnade in the rear; a lamp lights up the room.]

[CATILINE paces the floor back and forth; LENTULUS and CETHEGUS are with him.]

CATILINE. No, no! I say, you do not understand
Yourselves what you demand of me. Should I
Turn traitor and incite a civil war, —
Besmear my hand with Roman blood? No, no!
I'll never do it! Let the entire state
Condemn me if —

LENTULUS. You will not, Catiline?

CATILINE. No.

LENTULUS. Tell me, — have you nothing to avenge?
No insult? No one here you fain would strike?

CATILINE. Let him who will avenge; I shall not stir.
Yet silent scorn is likewise a revenge; —
And that alone shall be enough.

CETHEGUS. Aha, —
Our visit was, I see, inopportune.
Yet doubtless will the morrow bring you back
To other thoughts.

CATILINE. But why the morrow?

CETHEGUS. There are mysterious rumors in the air.
A vestal recently was led to death —

CATILINE. [Surprised.]
A vestal, — say you? Ah, what do you mean?

LENTULUS. Why, yes, a vestal. Many people murmur —

CATILINE. What do they murmur?

CETHEGUS. That in this dark affair
You are not altogether innocent.

CATILINE. This they believe of me?

LENTULUS. Such is the rumor;
Of course, — to us, to all your good old friends,
Such talk is trifling and of no account; —
The world, however, judges more severely.

CATILINE. [Deep in thought.] And is she dead?

CETHEGUS. Undoubtedly she is.
An hour's confinement in the convict tomb
Is quite enough —

LENTULUS. That is not our affair.
It was not therefore that we spoke of her.
But hear me, Catiline! Bethink yourself.
You sought the consulate; and all your welfare
Hung on that single fragile thread of hope.
Now is it sundered; everything is lost.

CATILINE. [Still deep in thought.]
"Vengeance you have invoked on your own head!"

CETHEGUS. Shake off these useless thoughts; they profit naught;
Act like a man; still can this fight be won;

A bold resolve now —; you have friends enough;
Speak but the word, and we shall follow you. —
You are not tempted? Answer!

CATILINE. No, I say!
And why are you so eager to conspire?
Be honest! Are you driven by thirst for freedom?
Is it in order to renew Rome's splendor
That you would ruin all?

LENTULUS. Indeed, 'tis not;
Yet surely is the hope of personal greatness
Sufficient motive for our enterprise!

CETHEGUS. And means enough to taste the joys of life
Are not, in truth, to be so lightly scorned.
That is my motive; — I am not ambitious.

CATILINE. I knew it. Only mean and paltry motives,
The hope of private vantage, urge you on.
No, no, my friends; I aimed at nobler things!
True, I have sought with bribes and promises
To seize ere now the consulate, and yet
My plan was greater and comprised much more
Than means like these would point to. Civic freedom,
The welfare of the state, — these were my aims.
Men have misjudged, appearances belied me;
My fate has willed it so. It must so be!

CETHEGUS. True; but the thought of all your many friends
Whom you can save from ruin and disgrace —?
You know, we shall ere long be driven to take
The beggars' staff because of our wild living.

  CATILINE. Then stop in season; that is my resolve.

LENTULUS. What, Catiline, — now you intend to change
Your mode of life? Ha, ha! you surely jest?

CATILINE. I am in earnest, — by the mighty gods!

CETHEGUS. Then there is nothing we can do with him.
Come, Lentulus, the others we'll inform
What answer he has given. We shall find
The merry company with Bibulus.

CATILINE. With Bibulus? How many a merry night
We have caroused at Bibulus' table!
Now is the tempest of my wild life ended;
Ere dawns the day I shall have left the city.

LENTULUS. What is all this?

CETHEGUS. You mean to go away?

CATILINE. This very night my wife and I together
Shall bid farewell to Rome forevermore.
In quiet Gaul we two shall found a home; —
The land I cultivate shall nourish us.

CETHEGUS. You will forsake the city, Catiline?

CATILINE. I will; I must! Disgrace here weighs me down.
Courage I have to bear my poverty,
But in each Roman face to read disdain
And frank contempt — ! No, no; that is too much!
In Gaul I'll live in quiet solitude;
There shall I soon forget my former self,
Dull all my longings for the greater things,
And as the vaguest dream recall the past.

LENTULUS. Then fare you well; may fortune follow you!

CETHEGUS. Remember us with kindness, Catiline,
As we shall you remember! To our brothers

We will relate this new and strange resolve.

    CATILINE. Then give them all a brother's hearty greeting!

    [LENTULUS and CETHEGUS leave.]

    [AURELIA has entered from the side, hut-stops frightened at the sight of those who are leaving; when they are gone she approaches CATILINE.]

AURELIA. [Gently reprimanding.]
Again these stormy comrades in your house?
O Catiline—!

CATILINE. This was their final visit.
I bade them all farewell. Now every bond
Forevermore is broken that bound me fast
And fettered me to Rome.

AURELIA. I've gathered up
Our bit of property. Not much perhaps;—
Yet, Catiline, enough for our contentment.

CATILINE. [Engrossed in thought.]
More than enough for me who squandered all.

AURELIA. Oh, brood no more on things we can not change;—
Forget what—

CATILINE. Happy he who could forget,—
Who could the memory tear from out his soul,
The many hopes, the goal of all desires.
Ah, time is needed ere I reach that state;
But I shall struggle—

AURELIA. I shall help you strive;
You shall be comforted for all your loss.

Yet we must leave as soon as possible.
Here life calls to you with a tempter's voice.
Is it not so, — we go this very night?

CATILINE. Yes, yes, — we leave this very night, Aurelia!

AURELIA. The little money left I've gathered up;
And for the journey it will be enough.

CATILINE. Good! I shall sell my sword and buy a spade.
What value henceforth is a sword to me?

AURELIA. You clear the land, and I shall till the soil.
Around our home will grow in floral splendor
A hedge of roses, sweet forget-me-nots,
The silent tokens of a chastened soul,
When as some youthful comrade you can greet
Each memory recurrent of the past.

CATILINE. That time, Aurelia? Ah, beloved, I fear —
That hour lies in a distant future's keeping.

CATILINE. [In a milder tone.]
But go, dear wife, and, while you may, repose.
Soon after midnight we shall start our journey.
The city then is lapped in deepest slumber,
And none shall guess our hidden destination.
The first glow in the morning sky shall find us
Far — far away; there in the laurel grove
We'll rest ourselves upon the velvet grass.

AURELIA. A new life opens up before us both —
Richer in happiness than this that's ended.
Now will I go. An hour's quiet rest
Will give me strength — . Good-night, my Catiline!

[She embraces him and goes out.]

CATILINE. [Gazes after her.]
Now is she gone! And I — what a relief!
Now can I cast away this wearisome
Hypocrisy, this show of cheerfulness,
Which least of all is found within my heart.
She is my better spirit. She would grieve
Were she to sense my doubt. I must dissemble.
Yet shall I consecrate this silent hour
To contemplation of my wasted life. —
This lamp, — ah, it disturbs my very thoughts; —
Dark it must be here, — dark as is my soul!

[He puts out the light; the moon shines through the pillars in the rear.]

CATILINE.
Too light, — yes, still too light! And yet, no matter; —
The pallid moonlight here does well befit
The twilight and the gloom that shroud my soul, —
Have ever shrouded all my earthly ways.

CATILINE. Hm, Catiline, then is this day your last;
Tomorrow morning you will be no longer
The Catiline you hitherto have been.
Distant in barren Gaul my life shall run
Its course, unknown as is a forest stream. —
Now am I wakened from those many visions
Of power, of greatness, of a life of deeds; —
They vanished like the dew; in my dark soul
They struggled long and died, — unseen of men.

CATILINE. Ah, it is not this dull and drowsy life,
Far from all mundane tumult, that affrights me.
If only for a moment I could shine,
And blaze in splendor like a shooting star, —
If only by a glorious deed I could

Immortalize the name of Catiline
With everlasting glory and renown, —
Then gladly should I, in the hour of triumph,
Forsake all things, — flee to a foreign strand; —
I'd plunge the dagger in my exiled heart,
Die free and happy; for I should have lived!

CATILINE. But oh, — to die without first having lived.
Can that be possible? Shall I so die?

[With uplifted hands.]

CATILINE. A hint, oh angry powers, — that it is
My fate to disappear from life forgotten,
Without a trace!

FURIA. [Outside behind the pillars.] It is not, Catiline!

CATILINE. [Taken aback.]
Who speaks? What warning voice is this I hear?
A spirit voice from out the underworld!

FURIA. [Comes forward in the moonlight.] I am your shadow.

CATILINE. [Terrified.] What, — the vestal's ghost!

FURIA. Deep must your soul have sunk if you recoil
From me!

CATILINE. Speak! Have you risen from the grave
With hatred and with vengeance to pursue me?

FURIA. Pursue you, — did you say? I am your shadow.
I must be with you wheresoe'er you go.

[She comes nearer.]

CATILINE. She lives! O gods, — then it is she, — no other,
No disembodied ghost.

FURIA. Or ghost or not, —
It matters little; I must follow you.

CATILINE. With mortal hate!

FURIA. Hate ceases in the grave,
As love and all the passions do that flourish
Within an earthly soul. One thing alone
In life and death remains unchangeable.

CATILINE. And what? Say forth!

FURIA. Your fate, my Catiline!

CATILINE. Only the gods of wisdom know my fate, —
No human being.

FURIA. Yet I know your fate.
I am your shadow; — strange, mysterious ties
Bind us together.

CATILINE. Bonds of hatred.

FURIA. No!
Rose ever spirit from the dankest grave
For hate and vengeance? Listen, Catiline!
The rivers of the underworld have quenched
Each earthly flame that raged within my breast.
As you behold me here, I am no longer
The stormy Furia, — wild and passionate, —
Whom once you loved —

CATILINE. You do not hate me then?

FURIA. Ah, now no more. When in the tomb I stood, —
And faltered on the path that separates

This life from death, at any moment ready
To greet the underworld, —lo, seized me then
An eerie shuddering; I know not what —;
I felt in me a mystic transformation; —
Away flowed hate, revenge, my very soul;
Each memory vanished and each earthly longing; —
Only the name of "Catiline" remains
Written in fiery letters on my heart.

CATILINE. Ah, wonderful! No matter who you are, —
A human form, a shadow from the dead, —
There lies withal a dreadful fascination
In your dark eyes, in every word you speak.

FURIA. Your mind is strong as mine; yet you give up,
Disheartened and irresolute, each hope
Of triumph and dominion. You forsake
The battlefield, where all your inmost plans
Could grow and blossom forth into achievement.

CATILINE. I must! Inexorable fate decrees it!

FURIA. Your fate? Why were you given a hero's strength, —
If not to struggle with what you call fate?

CATILINE. Oh, I have fought enough! Was not my life
A constant battle? What are my rewards?
Disgrace and scorn —!

FURIA. Ah, you are fallen low!
You struggle towards a high and daring goal,
Are eager to attain it; yet you fear
Each trifling hindrance.

CATILINE. Fear is not the reason.
The goal I sought is unattainable; —

The whole was but a fleeting dream of youth.

FURIA. Now you deceive yourself, my Catiline!
You hover still about that single project; —
Your soul is noble, — worthy of a ruler, —
And you have friends — . Ah, wherefore hesitate?

CATILINE. [Meditating.]
I shall — ? What do you mean — ? With civil blood — ?

FURIA. Are you a man, — yet lack a woman's courage?
Have you forgot that nimble dame of Rome,
Who sought the throne straight over a father's corpse?
I feel myself a Tullia now; but you — ?
Scorn and despise yourself, O Catiline!

CATILINE. Must I despise myself because my soul
No longer harbors selfish aspirations?

FURIA. You stand here at a cross-road in your life;
Yonder a dull, inactive course awaits you, —
A half-way something, neither sleep nor death; —
Before you, on the other hand, you see
A sovereign's throne. Then choose, my Catiline!

CATILINE. You tempt me and allure me to destruction.

FURIA. Cast but the die, — and in your hand is placed
Forevermore the welfare of proud Rome.
Glory and might your silent fate conceals,
And yet you falter, — dare not lift a hand!
You journey yonder to the forests, where
Each longing that you cherished will be quenched.
Ah, tell me, Catiline, is there no trace
Of thirst for glory left within your heart?
And must this princely soul, for triumphs born,

Vanish unknown in yonder nameless desert?
Hence, then! But know that thus you lose forever
What here you could by daring deeds attain.

   CATILINE. Go on, go on!

FURIA. With trembling and with fear
The future generations will recall
Your fate. Your life was all a daring game; —
Yet in the lustre of atonement it would shine,
Known to all men, if with a mighty hand
You fought your way straight through this surging
throng, —
If the dark night of thraldom through your rule
Gave way before a new-born day of freedom, —
If at some time you —

CATILINE. Hold! Ah, you have touched
The string that quivers deepest in my soul.
Your every word sounds like a ringing echo
Of what my heart has whispered day and night.

   FURIA. Now, Catiline, I know you once again!

CATILINE. I shall not go! You have recalled to life
My youthful zeal, my manhood's full-grown longings.
Yes, I shall be a light to fallen Rome, —
Daze them with fear like some erratic star!
You haughty wretches, — you shall soon discover
You have not humbled me, though for a time
I weakened in the heat of battle!

FURIA. Listen!
Whatever be the will of fate, — whatever
The mighty gods decree, we must obey.
Just so! My hate is gone; — fate thus decreed,
And so it had to be! Give me your hand
In solemn compact! — Ah, you hesitate?

You will not?

CATILINE. Will—? I gaze upon your eyes:
They flash,—like lightning in the gloom of night.
Now did you smile! Just so I've often pictured
Nemesis—

FURIA. What? Herself you wish to see,—
Then look within. Have you forgot your oath?

CATILINE. No, I remember;—yet you seem to me
A Nemesis—

FURIA. I am an image born
From your own soul.

CATILINE. [Meditating.] What is all this you say?
I sense but vaguely what I fail to grasp;
I glimpse mysterious, strangely clouded visions,—
But can not understand. I grope in darkness!

FURIA. It must be dark here. Darkness is our realm;—
In darkness is our rule. Give me your hand
In solemn pledge!

CATILINE. [Wildly.] O lovely Nemesis,—
My shadow,—image of my very soul,—
Here is my hand in everlasting compact.

[He seizes her hand violently; she looks at him with a stern smile.]

FURIA. Now we can never part!

CATILINE. Ah, like a stream
Of fire your touch went coursing through my veins!

'Tis blood no more that flows, but fiery flames; —
My breast now cabins and confines my heart;
My sight grows dull. Soon shall a flaming sea
Illumine with its light the Roman state!

[He draws his sword and brandishes it.]

CATILINE. My sword! My sword! Do you see how it flashes?
Soon will it redden in their tepid blood! —
What change is this in me? My brow burns hot;
A multitude of visions flit before me. —
Vengeance it is, — triumph for all those dreams
Of greatness, regal power, and lasting fame.
My watch-word shall be: livid flames and death!
The capitol! Now first I am myself!

[He rushes out; FURIA follows him.]

* * * * *

[The inside of a dimly illumined tavern.]

[STATILIUS, GABINIUS, COEPARIUS, and other young
ROMANS enter.]

STATILIUS. Here, comrades, we can while away the night;
Here we are safe; no one will overhear us.

GABINIUS. Ah, yes; now let us drink, carouse, enjoy!
Who knows how long it will be granted us?

STATILIUS. No, let us first await whatever tidings
Lentulus and Cethegus have for us.

GABINIUS. Bah, let them bring whatever news they will!
Meanwhile the wine is here; come, let us taste.
Quick, brothers, quick, — let's have a merry song!

[SERVANTS bring in wine and glasses.]

THE ASSEMBLED FRIENDS. (Sing.)

Bacchus, all praise to thee!
Joyful we raise to thee
Brimful the beaker!
Hail to thee, hail!
Wine, red and glowing,
Merrily flowing,
Drink of the wine-god, —
This be our song.

Gracious and friendly
Smiles father Liber;
Drunkenness waits us;
Clear is the wine.
Come, do not tarry!
Wine will make merry,
Joyful and airy,
Body and soul.

Thou above all the
Glittering bubbles,
Sparkling Falernian,
Glorious drink!
Courage and power,
These are your dower.
Gladsome the gift you
Bring to the soul.

Bacchus, all praise to thee!
Joyful we raise to thee
Brimful the beaker!
Hail to thee, hail!
Wine, red and glowing,
Merrily flowing,
Drink of the wine-god, —

This be our song.

[LENTULUS and CETHEGUS enter.]

LENTULUS. Cease all your song and merriment!

STATILIUS. What now?
Is Catiline not in your company?

GABINIUS. Surely he was quite willing?

COEPARIUS. Come, say forth!
What was his answer?

CETHEGUS. Ah, quite otherwise
Than we expected was his answer.

GABINIUS. Well?

LENTULUS. Well, all of our proposals he declined; —
He would not even hearken to our counsels.

STATILIUS. Is this the truth?

COEPARIUS. And wherefore would he not?

LENTULUS. In short, he will not. He forsakes his friends, —
Abandons us, — and leaves the city.

STATILIUS. What?
He leaves, you say?

CETHEGUS. 'Tis true; — he goes away
This very night. Yet, — blamed he can not be;
His ground was valid —

LENTULUS. Fear was his excuse!
In danger he forsakes us faithlessly.

GABINIUS. That is the friendship of our Catiline!

COEPARIUS. Never was Catiline faithless or afraid!

LENTULUS. And yet he leaves us now.

STATILIUS. Our hopes go with him.
Where's now the man to take the leadership?

COEPARIUS. He'll not be found; our plan we must forego.

LENTULUS. Not yet, not yet, my friends! First you shall hear
What I will say. Now what have we resolved?
That we should win at last by force of arms
What an unrighteous destiny denied.
Tyrants oppress us; — yet we wish to rule.
We suffer want; — yet wealth is our desire.

MANY VOICES. Yes, wealth and power! Wealth and power we
want!

LENTULUS. Yes, yes; we chose a comrade as our chief,
On whom there was no doubt we could rely.
Our trust he fails and turns his back to danger.
Ah, brothers, — be not daunted. He shall learn
We can succeed without him. What we need
Is some one man, fearless and resolute,
To take the lead —

SOME. Well, name us such a man!

LENTULUS. And should I name him, and should he comeforth, —
Will you then straightway choose him as your leader?

SOME. Yes, we will choose him!

OTHERS. Yes, we will, we will!

STATILIUS. Then name him, friend!

LENTULUS. Suppose it were myself?

GABINIUS. Yourself?

COEPARIUS. You, Lentulus—!

SEVERAL. [In doubt.] You wish to lead us?

LENTULUS. I do.

CETHEGUS. But can you? Such a task requires
The strength and courage of a Catiline.

LENTULUS. I do not lack the courage, nor the strength.
Each to his task! Or will you now turn back,
Now when the moment seems most opportune?
'Tis now or never! All things prophesy
Success for us—

STATILIUS. Good;—we will follow you!

OTHERS. We'll follow you!

GABINIUS. Well, now that Catiline
Forsakes our cause, you are no doubt the man
To lead us in our enterprise.

LENTULUS. Then hear
What plan of action I have outlined. First—

[CATILINE enters hastily.]

CATILINE. Here, comrades, here I am!

ALL. Catiline!

LENTULUS. He?
Oh, damned—

CATILINE. Speak out,—what do you ask of me?
Yet stay; I know already what it is.

I'll lead you on. Say — will you follow me?

ALL (EXCEPT LENTULUS). Yes, Catiline, — we follow if you lead!

STATILIUS. They have deceived us —

GABINIUS. — and belied your name!

COEPARIUS. They said you did intend to leave the city
And wash your hands completely of our cause.

CATILINE. Yes, so I did. Yet now no more; henceforth
Only for this great purpose do I live.

LENTULUS. What is this mighty purpose you proclaim?

CATILINE. My purpose here is higher than you think —
Perhaps than any thinks. Ah, hear me, friends!
First will I win to us each citizen
Who prizes liberty and values most
The public honor and his country's weal.
The spirit of ancient Rome is yet alive; —
The last faint spark is not yet wholly dead.
Now into brilliant flames it shall be fanned,
More glorious than ever flames before!
Alas, too long the stifling gloom of thraldom,
Dark as the night, lay blanketed on Rome.
Behold, — this realm — though proud and powerful
It seems — totters upon the edge of doom.
Therefore the stoutest hand must seize the helm.
Rome must be cleansed, — cleansed to the very roots;
The sluggish we must waken from their slumber, —
And crush to earth the power of these wretches
Who sow their poison in the mind and stifle
The slightest promise of a better life.
Look you, — 'tis civic freedom I would further, —
The civic spirit that in former times
Was regnant here. Friends, I shall conjure back
The golden age, when Romans gladly gave

Their lives to guard the honor of the nation,
And all their riches for the public weal!

LENTULUS. Ah, Catiline, you rave! Nothing of this
Had we in mind.

GABINIUS. What will it profit us
To conjure up again those ancient days
With all their dull simplicity?

SOME. No, no!
Might we demand —

OTHERS. — and means enough to live
A gay and carefree life!

  MANY VOICES. That is our aim!

COEPARIUS. Is it for others' happiness and freedom
We stake our lives upon a throw of dice?

  THE WHOLE GROUP. We want the spoils of victory!

CATILINE. Paltry race!
Are you the offspring of those ancient fathers?
To heap dishonor on your country's name, —
In such a way you would preserve its lustre!

LENTULUS. And you dare taunt us, — you who long since were
A terrifying token —

CATILINE. True, I was;
I was a terror to the good; and yet,
So paltry as you are was never I.

LENTULUS. Restrain your tongue; we brook no ridicule.

MANY. No, no, — we will not —

CATILINE. [Calmly.] So? You timid brood, —
You dare to think of doing something, — you?

LENTULUS. Ah, down with him!

MANY VOICES. Yes, down with Catiline!

[They draw their daggers and rush in on him; CATILINE calmly removes the cloak from his breast and regards them with a cold, scornful smile; they lower their daggers.]

CATILINE.
Thrust! Thrust! You dare not? Oh, my friends, my friends, —
I should respect you, if you plunged your daggers
In this uncovered bosom, as you threaten.
Is there no spark of courage in your souls?

SOME. He means our weal!

OTHERS. His taunts we have deserved.

CATILINE. You have, indeed. — Yet, see, — the hour is come
When you can wash away the blot of shame.
All that is of the past we will forget; —
A new existence is in store for us.

CATILINE. [With bitterness.]
Fool that I am! To stake success on you!
Burns any zeal within this craven mob?

CATILINE. [Carried away.]
Time was my dreams were glorious; great visions
Rushed through my mind or swept before my gaze.
I dreamed that, winged like Icarus of old,
I flew aloft beneath the vault of heaven;
I dreamed the gods endued my hands with strength
Of giants, offered me the lightning flash.

And this hand seized the lightning in its flight
And hurled it at the city far beneath.
And when the crimson flames lapped all, and rose
As Rome fell crumbling in a heap of ruins, —
Then called I with a loud and mighty voice,
And conjured Cato's comrades from the grave;
Thousands of spirits heard my call and came, —
Took life again — raised Rome from out her ashes.

[He breaks off.]

CATILINE. These were but dreams! Gods do not conjure up
The by-gone past into the light of day, —
And parted spirits never leave the grave.

CATILINE. [Wildly.] Is now this hand unable to restore
The ancient Rome, our Rome it shall destroy.
Where marble colonnades now towering stand,
Pillars of smoke through crackling flames shall whirl;
Then shall the Capitol crumble from its heights,
And palaces and temples sink to ruin!

CATILINE. Swear, comrades, that you dedicate your lives
To this great purpose! I shall take the lead.
Say, — will you follow me?

STATILIUS. We'll follow you!

[Several seem to be in doubt, and speak in whispers to one another. CATILINE regards them with a scornful smile.]

LENTULUS. [In an undertone.]
'Tis best we follow him. In sunken ruins
We're likeliest to realize our goal.

ALL. [Shouting.] Yes, Catiline; we'll all — all follow you!

CATILINE. Swear to me by the gods of our great sires
That you will heed my every nod!

THE WHOLE GROUP. [With uplifted hands.] Yes, yes;
We swear in all things blindly to obey!

CATILINE. Then singly steal your way, by different paths,
Into my house. Weapons you there will find.
I shall come later; you shall then discover
What plan of action I propose. Now go!

[They all go out.]

LENTULUS. [Detains CATILINE.]
A word! Know you the Allobrogian tribes
Have to the Senate sent ambassadors
With grievances and charges?

CATILINE. Yes, I know.
They came today into the city.

LENTULUS. Good.
What if we should attune them to our plans?
With them all Gaul will rise up in revolt;
And stir up strife against our enemies.

CATILINE. [Reluctant.]
Ah, we should seek barbarian allies?

LENTULUS. But such a league is a necessity.
With our own strength alone the fight is lost;
Help from without —

CATILINE. [With a bitter smile.] Ah, Rome is fallen low!
Her walls no longer harbor men with strength

Enough to overthrow a tottering ruin!

[They go out.]

* * * * *

[A garden to the rear of CATILINE's house, which is visible through the trees. To the left a side-building.]

[CURIUS, CETHEGUS, and OTHER CONSPIRATORS enter cautiously from the right in whispered conversation.]

CURIUS. But is it really true what you relate?

CETHEGUS. Yes, every word is true. A moment since
It was decided.

CURIUS. He takes charge of all?

CETHEGUS. Of everything. Just speak with him yourself.

[All, except CURIUS, enter the house.]

CURIUS. An eerie night! How all my thoughts are tossed
About in circles! Did I dream perchance?
Ah, real or fancied, — now I am awake, —
Whichever way I turn I see her form.

[CATILINE enters from the right.]

CATILINE. [Goes toward him.]
You here, my Curius? I have missed you much. —
My visit with the vestal took a turn
Quite unexpected —

CURIUS. [Confused.] So? Yes, you are right!

CATILINE. I shall no longer think of this affair.
It was a visit fraught with fate for me.

CATILINE. [Meditating.]
The furies, we are told, return at times

From the dark underworld to follow us
Through life forever. — Ah, if it were so!

CURIUS. [Uneasy.] What? Have you seen her — ?

CATILINE. She was here tonight. —
Yet let this be forgotten. Curius, listen, —
A weighty undertaking is on foot —

CURIUS. I know it all. Cethegus told me here —

CATILINE. Who knows what issue for this work the gods
Have set? Perchance it is my destiny
To perish now, crushed by malignant forces, —
And never reach my goal. Well, be it so!
But you, dear Curius, you whom I have loved
Since childhood, — you shall not be drawn within
This fateful maelstrom. Promise me, — remain
Within the city if I elsewhere choose
To open my attack, — which is quite likely;
Nor aid us till success has crowned our work.

CURIUS. [Moved.]
Oh, what a friend and father! All this care — !

CATILINE. You promise this? Then here we say farewell;
Wait but a moment; I shall soon return.

[He goes into the house.]

CURIUS. [Gazing after him.]
He loves me still. Of naught is he distrustful.

[LENTULUS and OTHER CONSPIRATORS enter from the right.]

LENTULUS. Ah, Curius, did not Catiline just now
Pass through the garden?

CURIUS. Yes, he is within.

[They go into the house.]

CURIUS. [Paces about uneasy.]
How shall I curb this longing in my soul?
There is a restless turmoil in my blood.
Ah, Furia,—what a strange, mysterious woman!
Where are you? When shall I see your face again?

CURIUS. Where has she fled? Ah, shadow-like she slipped
Away, when I had freed her from the grave.
And those mysterious, prophetic words,—
And more, her eyes, gleaming at once and dimmed—!
What if it were but madness? Has the grave
With all its terror darkened—?

FURIA. [Behind him among the trees.] No, pale youth!

CURIUS. [With a cry.] My Furia! You—?

FURIA. [Comes nearer.] Here dwells Catiline.
Where he is,—there must Furia also be.

CURIUS. Oh, come with me, beloved. I shall lead
You into safety. Think—if some one saw you!

FURIA. The dead need have no fear. Have you forgotten—
You took my corpse and brought it from the grave?

CURIUS. Again those terrifying words! Oh, hear me;—
Come to your senses,—come with me away!

[He tries to seize her hand.]

FURIA. [Thrusts him wildly back.]
You reckless fool,—do you not shrink with fear
Before this child of death, but risen up

70

A fleeting moment from the underworld?

CURIUS. Before you now I fear. And yet this fear,
This strange, mysterious dread, is my delight.

FURIA. What would you me? In vain is all your pleading.
I'm of the grave, and yonder is my home; —
With dawn's approach I must again be speeding
Back to the vale of shadows whence I come.
You doubt me, — do not think that I have sat
Among the pallid shades in Pluto's hall?
I tell you, I was even now below, —
Beyond the river and the gloomy marshes.

CURIUS. Then lead me there!

FURIA. You?

CURIUS. I shall gladly follow,
Though you should lead me through the jaws of death!

FURIA. It cannot be! On earth we two must part; —
Yonder the dead and living dare not meet. —

FURIA. Why do you rob me of my fleeting moments?
I've but the hours of night in which to work;
My task is of the night; I am its herald.
But where is Catiline?

CURIUS. Ah, him you seek?

FURIA. Yes, him I seek.

CURIUS. Then him you still pursue?

FURIA. Why rose I from the spirit underworld
Tonight, if not because of Catiline?

CURIUS. Alas, this fury that has seized your soul —!
Yet you are lovely even in your madness.
Oh, Furia, think no more of Catiline!
Come, flee with me! Command me, — I shall serve you!

[He prostrates himself before her.]

CURIUS. A prostrate slave I here entreat of you
One single look. Oh, hear me, Furia, hear me!
I love but you! A sweet and lethal fire
Consumes my soul, and you — ah, you alone —
Can ease my suffering. —

FURIA. [Looks towards the house.] Yonder there's a light —
And many men. What now is going on
Within the house of Catiline?

CURIUS. [Jumps up.] Again
This name! Around him hover all your thoughts.
Oh, I could hate him —!

FURIA. Has he then resolved
To launch at last the daring enterprise
He long has cherished?

CURIUS. Then you know — ?

FURIA. Yes, all.

CURIUS. Ah, then you doubtless know, too, he himself
Is foremost in this daring enterprise?
Yet, I adjure you, beg you, think no more
Of Catiline!

FURIA. Answer me this alone;
'Tis all I ask of you. Do you go with him?

CURIUS. He is to me a tender father —

FURIA. [Smiling.] He?
My Catiline?

CURIUS. Ah!

FURIA. He, — round whom my thoughts
Course without rest?

CURIUS. My brain is in a tumult —
I hate this man —! Oh, I could murder him!

FURIA. Did you not lately swear you were prepared
To do my bidding?

CURIUS. Ask me what you will;
In everything I serve you and obey!
I only beg, — forget this Catiline.

FURIA. I shall forget him first — when he has stepped
Into his grave.

CURIUS. [Draws back.] Ah, you demand that I —?

FURIA. You need not use the steel; you can betray
His enterprise —

CURIUS. Murder and treachery
At once! Remember, Furia, he is still
My foster-father and —

FURIA. — My aim in life!
Ah, timid fool, — so you dare speak of love, —
Who lack the fortitude to strike him down

That stands across your path? Away from me!

[She turns her back on him.]

CURIUS. [Holding her back.]
No; — do not leave me! I am in all things willing!
A shudder chills me as I look on you;
And yet I cannot break this net asunder
Wherein you trapped my soul.

FURIA. Then you are willing?

CURIUS. Why do you mock me with such questioning?
If I am willing? Have I any will?
Your gaze is like the serpent's when 'tis fixed
With magic power upon the bird, that circles
Wildly about in terror-stricken awe,
Drawn ever nearer to the dreadful fangs.

FURIA. Then to your task!

CURIUS. And when I've sacrificed
My friendship to my love for you, — what then?

FURIA. I shall forget that Catiline existed.
Then will my task be ended. Ask no more!

CURIUS. For this reward I should — ?

FURIA. You hesitate?
Is then your hope so faint that you forget
What gifts a grateful woman can bestow,
When first the time — ?

CURIUS. By all the powers of night, —
I'll not delay! He only stands between us.
Then let him perish! Quenched is every spark
Of feeling for him; every bond is sundered! —

Who are you, lovely vision of the night?
Near you I'm turned to marble, burned to ashes.
My longing chills me, — terror fires the soul;
My love is blended hate and sorcery.
Who am I now? I know myself no more;
One thing I know; I am not he I was,
Ere you I saw. I'll plunge into the deep
To follow you! Doomed — doomed is Catiline!
I'll to the Capitol. This very night
The senate is assembled. Then farewell!
A written note betrays his enterprise.

[He goes out hastily.]

FURIA. [To herself.]
The heavens grow dark; soon will the lightning play.
The end is fast approaching, Catiline; —
With measured steps you journey to your grave!

[The Allobrogian ambassadors, AMBIORIX and OLLOVICO, come out of the house without noticing FURIA, who stands half concealed in the shade between the trees.]

AMBIORIX. So then it is decided! Venturesome
It was to enter into such a compact.

OLLOVICO. True;
Yet their refusal of each righteous claim
Opens no other way to liberty.
The prize of victory, — should our friends succeed, —
Outweighs indeed the perils of the conflict
That now awaits us.

AMBIORIX. Brother, so it is!

OLLOVICO. Emancipation from the rule of Rome, —
Freedom long lost is surely worth a struggle.

AMBIORIX. Now we must hasten homeward with all speed,
Kindling through Gaul the flames of insurrection.
It will be easy to persuade the tribes
To 'rise up in revolt; they'll follow us
And join the partisans of Catiline.

OLLOVICO. Hard will the fight be; mighty still is Rome.

AMBIORIX. It must be risked. Come, Ollovico, come!

FURIA. [Calls warningly to them.] Woe unto you!

AMBIORIX. [Startled.] By all the gods!

OLLOVICO. [Terrified.] Ah, hear!
A voice cries warning to us in the dark!

FURIA. Woe to your people!

OLLOVICO. Yonder stands she, brother, —
The pale and ill-foreboding shadow. See!

FURIA. Woe unto all who follow Catiline!

AMBIORIX. Home, home! Away! We'll break all promises!

OLLOVICO. A voice has warned us, and we shall obey.

[They go out hurriedly to the right.]

[CATILINE comes out of the house in the background.]

CATILINE. Ah, desperate hope — to think of crushing Rome
With such a host of cowards and poltroons!
What spurs them on? With frankness they confess —
Their only motive is their want and greed.
Is it then worth the trouble for such aims
To shed men's blood? And what have I to win?
What can I gain?

FURIA. [Invisible among the trees.] Revenge, my Catiline!

CATILINE. [Startled.]
Who speaks! Who wakes the spirit of revenge
From slumber? Came this voice then from the deep
Within my soul? Revenge? Yes, that's the word, —
My watch-word and my battle-cry. Revenge!
Revenge for all the hopes and all the dreams
Which ever a vindictive fate destroyed!
Revenge for all my years of wasted life!

[The CONSPIRATORS come armed out of the house.]

LENTULUS. Still rest the shades of darkness on the city.
Now is it time to break away.

SEVERAL. [Whispering.] Away!

[AURELIA comes out of the side-building without noticing the
CONSPIRATORS.]

AURELIA. Beloved, — are you here?

CATILINE. [With a cry.] Aurelia!

AURELIA. Say, —
Have you been waiting for me?

[She becomes aware of the Conspirators and rushes to him.]

AURELIA. Gracious gods!

CATILINE. [Thrusts her aside.] Woman, away from me!

AURELIA. Speak, Catiline!
These many men in arms — ? And you as well — ?
Oh, you will go —

CATILINE. [Wildly.] Yes, by the spirits of night, —
A merry journey! See — this flashing sword!
It thirsts for blood! I go — to quench its thirst.

AURELIA. My hope, — my dream! Ah, blissful was my dream!
Thus am I wakened from my dreaming —

CATILINE. Silence!
Stay here, — or follow! But my heart is cold
To tears and lamentations. — Friends, behold
How bright the full moon in the west declines!
When next that full moon in its orient shines,
An avalanche of fire shall sweep the state
And all its golden glory terminate.
A thousand years from now, when it shall light
Mere crumbling ruins in the desert night, —
One pillar in the dust of yonder dome
Shall tell the weary wanderer: Here stood Rome!

[He rushes out to the right; all follow him.]

* * * * *

THIRD ACT

[CATILINE's camp in a wooded field in Etruria. To the right is seen CATILINE's tent and close by it an old oak tree. A camp fire is burning outside the tent; similar fires are to be seen among the trees in the background. It is night. At intervals the moon breaks through the clouds.]

[STATILIUS lies stretched out asleep by the camp fire.
MANLIUS paces back and forth in front of the tent.]

MANLIUS. Such is the way of young and buoyant souls.
They slumber on as peaceful and secure
As though embosomed in their mothers' arms,
Instead of in a forest wilderness.
They rest as though they dream some merry game
Were held in store for them when they awake,
Instead of battle, — the last one, perchance,
That will be theirs to fight.

STATILIUS. [Awakes and rises.] Still standing guard?
You must be weary? I'll relieve you now.

MANLIUS. Go rest yourself instead. Youth needs his sleep;
His untamed passions tax his native strength.
'Tis otherwise when once the hair turns gray,
When in our veins the blood flows lazily,
And age weighs heavily upon our shoulders.

STATILIUS. Yes, you are right. Thus I too shall in time,
An old and hardened warrior —

MANLIUS. Are you sure
The fates decreed you such a destiny?

STATILIUS. And pray, why not? Why all these apprehensions?
Has some misfortune chanced?

MANLIUS. You think no doubt
That we have naught to fear, foolhardy youth?

STATILIUS. Our troops are strongly reenforced —

MANLIUS. Indeed, —
With fugitive slaves and gladiators —

STATILIUS. Well, —
Grant that they are; together they may prove
No little aid, and all the tribes of Gaul
Will send us help —

MANLIUS. — Which has not yet arrived.

STATILIUS. You doubt that the Allobroges will keep
Their promised word?

MANLIUS. I know these people well
From days gone by. However, let that pass.
The day that dawns will doubtless bring to light
What destinies the gods have set for us.

MANLIUS. But go the rounds, my friend, and ascertain
If all the guards perform their proper tasks.
For we must fend against a night attack;
We know not where the enemy makes his stand.

[STATILIUS goes into the forest.]

MANLIUS. [Alone by the camp fire.]
The clouds begin to gather thick and fast;
It is a dark and storm-presaging night; —
A misty fog hangs heavy on my breast,
As though foreboding mishap to us all.
Where is it now, that easy carefree spirit
With which in former times I went to war?
Ah, can it be the weight of years alone
That now I feel? Strange — strange, indeed, — last night
Even the young seemed sorely out of heart.

MANLIUS. [After a pause.]
The gods shall know revenge was not the aim
For which I joined and followed Catiline.
My wrath flared up within me for a space
When first I felt I had been wronged, insulted; —
The old blood is not yet entirely cold;
Now and again it courses warmly through my veins.
But the humiliation is forgotten.
I followed Catiline for his own sake;
And I shall watch o'er him with zealous care.
Here stands he all alone amidst these hosts
Of paltry knaves and dissolute companions.
They cannot comprehend him, — he in turn
Is far too proud to wish to fathom them.

[He throws some branches on the fire and remains standing in silence. CATILINE comes out of the tent.]

CATILINE. [To himself.]
Midnight approaches. Everything is hushed; —
Only to my poor eyes sleep fails to come.
Cold is the night wind; 'twill refresh my soul
And give me strength anew —. I sorely need it!

[He becomes aware of MANLIUS.]

CATILINE. 'Tis you, old Manlius? And do you stand guard
Alone on such a night?

MANLIUS. Oft have I stood
Guard over you in childhood's early days.
Say, do you not recall?

CATILINE. Those days are gone;
With them, my peace; wherever now I go,
I'm haunted by a multitude of visions.
All things find shelter in my bosom, Manlius; —
Save peace alone. That — that is far away.

MANLIUS. Cast off these gloomy thoughts and take your rest!
Remember that the morrow may require
Your utmost strength for our deliverance.

CATILINE. I cannot rest. If I but close my eyes
One fleeting moment in forgetful slumber,
I'm tossed about in strange, fantastic dreams.
Here on my couch I lay now, half asleep,
When these same visions reappeared again,
More strange than ever, — more mysterious
And puzzling —. Ah, if I could only know
What this forebodes! But no —

MANLIUS. Confide your dream
To me. Perhaps I can expound its meaning.

CATILINE. [After a pause.]
If I slept or if I waked, scarcely can I say;
Visions fast pursued each other in a mad array.
Soon a deepening twilight settles over everything;
And a night swoops down upon me on her wide-spread wing,
Terrible and dark, unpierced, save by the lightning's flare;
I am in a grave-like dungeon, filled with clammy air.

Lofty is the ceiling and with thunderclouds o'ercast;
Multitudes of shadow forms go racing wildly past,
Whirl around in roaring eddies, as the ocean wave
Draws the raging storm and breaks against a rocky cave.
Yet amid this frenzied tumult children often come,
Decked in flowers, singing of a half-forgotten home.
Soon the darkness round them changes to a vivid glare, —
Dimly in the center I descry a lonely pair;
Ah, two women, — stern the one and gloomy as the night, —
And the other gentle, like the evening in its flight.
How familiar to my eyes the two lone figures seemed!
With her smiling countenance the one upon me beamed;
Like the zigzag lightning flashed the other's piercing eye;
Terror seized my soul, — yet on I gazed in ecstasy.
Proudly upright stands the one, the other leans in weariness
On the solitary table, where they play a game of chess.
Pawns they barter, or they move them now from place to place; —
Then the game is lost and won, — she fades away in space, —
She who radiantly smiled, ah, she who lost the game;
Instantly the bands of children vanish whence they came.
Tumult rises; darkness deepens; but from out the night
Two eyes fix upon me, in a victor's gloating right;
Then my brain reels; I see nothing but those baleful eyes.
But what else I dreamed of in that frenzied slumber lies
Far within me hidden, buried deep beyond recall.
Could I but remember. Gone forever is it all.

MANLIUS. Remarkable, indeed, my Catiline,
Is this your dream.

CATILINE. [Meditating.] If I could but remember —
But no; my memory fails me —

MANLIUS. Brood no longer
Upon these thoughts. For what are dreams, indeed,
But pale chimeras only, darkling visions,

On nothing founded, and by naught explained?

CATILINE. Yes, you are right; I will no longer brood; —
Already I am calm. But go your way;
You need some rest. The meanwhile I shall walk
In privacy and meditate my plans.

[MANLIUS goes into the forest.]

CATILINE. [Paces for some time back and forth by the camp fire, which is about to go out; then he stops and speaks thoughtfully.] If I could only —. Ah, it is unmanly To brood and be distressed by thoughts like these. And yet, — here in the stillness of the night, This lonely solitude, again I see Rising before me life-like all I dreamed.

[A SHADOW, attired like an old warrior in armor and toga, stems to rise from the earth among the trees a short distance from him.]

CATILINE. [Recoils before THE SHADOW.]
Great powers of heaven — !

THE SHADOW. Greetings, Catiline!

CATILINE. What will you have? Who are you, pallid shade?

THE SHADOW. One moment! It is here my right to question, —
And you shall answer. Do you no longer know
This voice from ages long since passed away?

CATILINE. Methinks I do; yet certain I am not —.
But speak, whom seek you at this midnight hour?

THE SHADOW. 'Tis you I seek. Know that this hour alone
Is granted me as respite here on earth.

CATILINE. By all the gods! Who are you? Speak!

THE SHADOW. Be calm!
Hither I come to call you to account.
Why do you envy me the peace of death?
Why do you drive me from my earthy dwelling?
Why do you mar my rest with memories,
That I must seek you, whisper menaces,
To guard the honor I so dearly bought?

CATILINE. Alas! this voice—! Somehow I seem to know—

THE SHADOW. What is there left of my imperial power?
A shadow like myself; yes, scarcely that.
Both sank into the grave—and came to naught.
'Twas dearly bought; dear, dear was it attained.
For it I sacrificed all peace in life,
And waived all claims to peace beyond the grave.
And now you come and want to wrest from me
With daring hands what little I have left.
Are there not paths enough to noble deeds?
Why must you choose the one that I have chosen?
I gave up everything in life to power;
My name—so dreamed I—should forever stand,
Not beaming like a star with friendly lustre,—
No, like a flash against the midnight sky!
I did not covet fame, the goal of hundreds,
For magnanimity and noble deeds;
Nor admiration;—far too many share
That fate already: so will many more
Until the end of time. Of blood and horror
I wished to build me my renown and fame.
With silent dread, as on some meteor
That now appears in mystery and is gone
Again,—men should gaze back upon my life,
And look askance on me, whom no one ever,
Before or since then, dared to emulate.
Yes, thus I dreamed and dreamed,—and was deceived.
Why did I not surmise, when you stood near me,
The secret thoughts then growing in your soul.
Yet, Catiline, beware; know that I see

Beyond the veil that hides from you the future.
Written among the stars—I read your fate!

    CATILINE. You read my fate? Expound it then to me!

THE SHADOW. No, first beyond death's gloomy gate
  Shall fade away the mists that hide
  The gruesome and the nobly great,
  Borne ever on by time and tide.
  This from thy book of fate alone
  A liberated soul may tell thee:
  Perish thou shalt by deed thine own,
  And yet a stranger's hand shall fell thee.

    [THE SHADOW glides away as in a mist.]

CATILINE. [After a pause.]
Ah, he has vanished. Was it but a dream?
No, no; even here he stood; the moonbeams played
Upon his sallow visage. Yes, I knew him!
It was the man of blood, the old dictator,
Who sallied from his grave to frighten me.
He feared lest he should lose the victor's crown,—
Not the reward of honor, but the terror
Whereby his memory lives. Are bloodless shades
Spurred onward also by the thought of glory?

    [Paces to and fro uneasily.]

CATILINE. All things storm in upon me. Now Aurelia
In gentle admonition speaks,—and now
In me reëchoes Furia's warning cry.
Nay, more than that;—out of the grave appear
The pallid shadows of a by-gone age.
They threaten me. I should now stop and pause?
I should turn back? No. I shall venture on
Unfaltering;—the victory soon is mine!

    [CURIUS comes through the forest in great agitation.]

CURIUS. O Catiline—!

CATILINE. [Surprised.] What, you,—you here, my friend!

CURIUS. I had to—

CATILINE. Wherefore staid you not in town?

CURIUS. Fear prompted me; I had to seek you here.

CATILINE. You rush for my sake blindly into danger.
You thoughtless lad! Yet, come into my arms!

[Moves to embrace him.]

CURIUS. [Draws back.]
No! Do not touch me! Do not even come near me!

CATILINE. What ails you, my dear Curius?

CURIUS. Up! Break camp!
Flee, if you can, even this very hour!
On every highway come the enemy troops;
Your camp is being surrounded.

CATILINE. Calm yourself;
You rave. Speak, has the journey shaken you—?

CURIUS. Oh no; but save yourself while there is time!
You are betrayed—

[Prostrates himself before him.]

CATILINE. [Starts back.] Betrayed! What are you saying?

CURIUS. Betrayed by one in friendly guise!

CATILINE. You err;
These stormy friends are loyal even as you.

CURIUS. Then woe to you for all their loyalty!

CATILINE. Compose yourself! It is your love for me,
Your interest in my safety, that has wakened
Imaginary dangers in your mind.

CURIUS. Oh, do you know these words do murder me?
But flee! I do entreat you earnestly —

CATILINE. Be calm and speak your mind. Why should I flee?
The enemy knows not where I make my stand.

CURIUS. Indeed he does, — he knows your every plan!

CATILINE. What, are you mad? He knows —? Impossible!

CURIUS. Oh, were it so! But use the hour remaining;
Still you may save yourself perhaps in flight!

CATILINE. Betrayed? No, — ten times no; impossible!

CURIUS. [Seizes his dagger and holds it out to him.]
Catiline, plunge this dagger in my bosom; —
Straight through the heart! 'Twas I betrayed your plans!

CATILINE. You? What madness!

CURIUS. Yes, it was in madness!
Ask not the reason; scarce I know myself;
I say, — I have revealed your every counsel.

CATILINE. [In bitter grief.]
Now have you killed my faith in sacred friendship!

CURIUS. Oh, send the dagger home, and torture me
No longer with forbearance —!

CATILINE. [Kindly.] Live, my Curius!
Arise! You erred; — but I forgive you all.

CURIUS. [Overcome.]
O Catiline, my heart is crushed with grief — !
But hasten; flee! There is no time to tarry.
Soon will the Roman troops invade your camp;
They're under way; on every side they come.

   CATILINE. Our comrades in the city — ?

CURIUS. They are captured; —
Some were imprisoned, most of them were killed!

   CATILINE. [To himself.] What fate — what fate!

CURIUS. [Again holds out the dagger to him.]
Then plunge it in my heart!

CATILINE. [Looks at him calmly.] No, you were but a tool.
You acted well —

   CURIUS. Oh, let me die and expiate my sin!

   CATILINE. I have forgiven you.

CATILINE. [As he goes.] But one thing now
Is there to choose!

   CURIUS. [Jumps up.] Yes, flight!

   CATILINE. Heroic death!

   [He goes away through the forest.]

CURIUS. 'Tis all in vain! Ruin awaits him here.
This mildness is a tenfold punishment!
I'll follow him; one thing I shall be granted: —
To perish fighting by the hero's side!

[He rushes out. LENTULUS and TWO GLADIATORS come stealing among the trees.]

LENTULUS. [Softly.] Some one was speaking —

ONE OF THE GLADIATORS. Aye, but now all's quiet.

THE OTHER GLADIATOR. Perchance it was the sentinel relieved
Of duty.

LENTULUS. That may be. This is the place;
Here shall you wait. Are both your weapons sharp,
Ground for their purpose?

THE FIRST GLADIATOR. Bright as is the lightning!

THE SECOND GLADIATOR.
Mine, too, cuts well. In the last Roman games
Two gladiators died beneath this sword.

LENTULUS. Then stand you ready in this thicket here.
And when a man, whom I shall designate,
Goes toward the tent, then shall you rush out quick
And strike him from behind.

THE FIRST GLADIATOR. It shall be done!

[Both GLADIATORS conceal themselves; LENTULUS goes spying around.]

LENTULUS. [To himself.]
It is a daring game I here attempt; —
Yet must it be performed this very night,
If done at all. — If Catiline should fall,
No one can lead them on except myself;
I'll purchase them with golden promises,
And march without delay upon the city,
Where still the senate, struck with panic fear,
Neglects to arm itself against the danger.

[He goes in among the trees.]

THE FIRST GLADIATOR. [Softly to the other.]
Who is this stranger we must fall upon?

THE SECOND GLADIATOR. What matters it to us who he may be?
Lentulus pays our hire; the blame is his:
He must himself defend the act we do.

LENTULUS. [Returns quickly.]
Stand ready now; the man we wait is coming!

[LENTULUS and the GLADIATORS lie in wait among the bushes.]

[Soon after, CATILINE comes through the forest and goes toward the tent.]

LENTULUS. [Whispering.]
Out! Fall upon him! Strike him from behind!

[All three rush on CATILINE.]

CATILINE. [Draws his sword and defends himself.]
Ah, scoundrels, — do you dare to — ?

LENTULUS. [To the GLADIATORS.] Cut him down!

CATILINE. [Recognizes him.]
You, Lentulus, would murder Catiline?

THE FIRST GLADIATOR. [Terrified.] He it is!

THE SECOND GLADIATOR. [Draws back.] Catiline! I'll never use
The sword on him. Come flee!

[Both GLADIATORS make their escape.]

LENTULUS. Then die by mine!

[They fight; CATILINE strikes the sword from the hand of Lentulus; the latter tries to escape, but CATILINE holds him fast.]

CATILINE. Murderer! Traitor!

LENTULUS. [Entreating.] Mercy, Catiline!

CATILINE. I spell your plans upon your countenance.
You wished to murder me, and put yourself
Into the chieftain's place. Was it not so?

LENTULUS. Yes, Catiline, it was even so!

CATILINE. [Looks at him with repressed scorn.] What then?
If 'tis the power you want, — so let it be!

LENTULUS. Explain, — what do you mean?

CATILINE. I shall resign;
And you may lead the army —

LENTULUS. [Surprised.] You resign?

CATILINE. I shall. But be prepared for all events;
Know this — our undertaking is revealed:
The senate is informed of every plan;
Its troops hem us about —

LENTULUS. What do you say?

CATILINE. Now shall I call a council of our friends;
Do you come too, — announce your leadership;
I shall resign.

LENTULUS. [Detains him.] One moment, Catiline!

CATILINE. Your time is precious; ere the dawn of day
You may expect an onslaught —

LENTULUS. [Anxiously.] Hear me, friend!
Surely you jest? It is impossible —

CATILINE. Our project, I have told you, is betrayed.
Show now your firmness and sagacity!

   LENTULUS. Betrayed? Then woe to us!

CATILINE. [Smiles scornfully.] You paltry coward!
You tremble *now*; — yet *you* would murder *me*;
You think a man like you is called to rule?

   LENTULUS. Forgive me, Catiline!

CATILINE. Make your escape
By hurried flight, if still it can be done.

   LENTULUS. Ah, you permit me then — ?

CATILINE. And did you think
It was my purpose to forsake this post
In such an hour as this? You little know me.

   LENTULUS. O, Catiline — !

CATILINE. [Coldly.] Waste not your moments here!
Seek your own safety; — I know how to die.

   [He turns away from him.]

LENTULUS. [To himself.]
I thank you for these tidings, Catiline; —
I shall make use of them to serve my end.
'Twill stand me in good stead now that I know
This region well; I'll seek the hostile army
And guide it hitherward by secret paths,
To your destruction and to my salvation. —
The serpent that you trample in the dust

So arrogantly still retains its sting!

[He goes.]

CATILINE. [After a pause.]
This is the trust I built my hopes upon!
Thus one by one they leave me. Oh ye gods!
Treason and cowardice alone stir up
The sullen currents of their slavish souls.
Oh, what a fool am I with all my hopes!
I would destroy yon viper's nest, that Rome, —
Which is long since a heap of sunken ruins.

[The sound of arms is heard approaching; he listens.]

CATILINE. They come, they come! Still are there valiant men
Among them. Ah, the joyous clang of steel!
The merry clash of shields against each other!
Anew the fire kindles in my breast;
The reckoning is near, — the mighty hour
That settles every doubt. I hail the day!

[MANLIUS, STATILIUS, GABINIUS, and many OTHER CON-
SPIRATORS come through the forest.]

MANLIUS. Here, Catiline, come your friends and comrades true;
In camp I spread the alarm, as you commanded —

CATILINE. And have you told them — ?

MANLIUS. Yes, — they know our plight.

STATILIUS. We know it well, and we shall follow you
With sword in hand to fight for life and death.

CATILINE. I thank you all, my comrades brave in arms!
But do not think, my friends, that life or death
Is ours to choose; — our only choice is this:
Death in heroic battle with the foe,

Or death by torture when like savage beasts
We shall be hounded down relentlessly.
Ah, which do you prefer? To risk in flight
A wretched life prolonged in misery,
Or like your proud and worthy sires of old
To perish nobly on the battlefield?

GABINIUS. We choose to fight and die!

MANY VOICES. Lead us to death!

CATILINE. Then let us be off! Through death we shall achieve
The glorious life of immortality.
Our fall, our name, through distant generations
Shall be proclaimed with lofty pride—

FURIA. [Calls out behind him among the trees.] —O terror!

SOME VOICES. Behold,—a woman—!

CATILINE. [Startled.] Furia! You—you here?
What brought you here?

FURIA. Ah, I must lead you on
To your great goal.

CATILINE. Where is my goal, then? Speak!

FURIA. Each mortal seeks his goal in his own way.
And you seek yours through ever hopeless strife;
The struggle yields defeat and certain death.

CATILINE. Yet also honor and immortal fame!
Go, woman! Great and noble is this hour!
My heart is closed against your raucous cries.

[AURELIA appears in the door of the tent.]

AURELIA. My Catiline—!

[She stops, terrified at the sight of the throng.]

CATILINE. [Painfully.] Aurelia,—oh, Aurelia!

AURELIA. What is the trouble? All this stir in camp—
What is on foot here?

CATILINE. You I could forget!
What will your fate be now—?

FURIA. [Whispers scornfully, unnoticed by AURELIA.]
Ah, Catiline,
Already wavering in your high resolve?
Is this your death defiance?

CATILINE. [Flaring up.] No, by the gods!

AURELIA. [Comes nearer.]
Oh, speak, beloved! Keep me in doubt no longer—

FURIA. [In an undertone behind him.]
Flee with your wife—the while your comrades die!

MANLIUS. Tarry no longer; lead us out to battle—

CATILINE. Oh, what a choice! And yet,—here is no choice;—
I must go on,—I dare not stop midway.

CATILINE. [Calls out.] Then follow me to battle on the plain!

AURELIA. [Throws herself in his arms.]
Catiline,—do not leave me,—take me with you!

CATILINE. No, stay, Aurelia!

FURIA. [As before.] Take her, Catiline!
Worthy your death will be, as was your life,
When you are vanquished—in a woman's arms!

CATILINE. [Thrusts AURELIA aside.]
Away, you who would rob me of my fame!
Death shall o'ertake me in the midst of men.
I have a life to atone, a name to clear—

FURIA. Just so; just so, my gallant Catiline!

CATILINE. All things I will uproot from out my soul
That bind me to my life of empty dreams!
All that is of the past shall henceforth be
As if 'twere not—

AURELIA. Oh, cast me not away!
By all the love I bear you, Catiline,—
I beg you, I adjure,—let us not part!

CATILINE. My heart is dead, my sight is blind to love.
From life's great mockery I turn my eyes;
And gaze but on the dim, yet mighty star
Of fame that is to be!

AURELIA. O gods of mercy!

[She leans faint against the tree outside the tent.]

CATILINE. [To the Warriors.] And now away!

MANLIUS. The din of arms I hear!

SEVERAL VOICES. They come, they come.

CATILINE. Good! We will heed their warning.
Long was our night of shame; our dawn is near—.
To battle in the crimson sky of morning!
By Roman sword, with Roman fortitude,
The last of Romans perish in their blood!

[They rush out through the forest; a great alarm, rent with battle-cries, is heard from within the camp.]

FURIA. He is gone forever. My great task in life is done.
Cold and rigid we shall find him in the morning sun.

AURELIA. [Aside.]
In his passion-glutted bosom then should love no longer dwell?
Was it nothing but a dream? His angry words I heard full well.

FURIA. Hark, the weapons clash; already at the brink
of death he stands;
Soon a noiseless shadow he will hasten toward the spirit
lands.

AURELIA. [Startled.]
Who are you, prophetic voice, that yonder comes to me,
Like the night-owl's cry of warning from some far-off tree!
Are you from the clammy underworld of spirits come
Hence to lead my Catiline into your gloomy home?

FURIA. Home is ay the journey's goal, and all his wanderings lay
Through the reeking swamps of life —

AURELIA. But only for a day.
Free and noble was his heart, his spirit strong and true,
Till around it serpent-like a poisoned seedling grew.

FURIA.
So the plane-tree, too, keeps fresh and green its leafy dress,
Till its trunk is smothered in a clinging vine's caress.

AURELIA.
Now did you betray your source. For time and time again
Echoed from the lips of Catiline this one refrain.
You the serpent are, who poisoned all my joy in life,
Steeled his heart against my kindness through your deadly strife.
From those waking night-dreams well I know your infamy,

Like a threat I see you stand between my love and me.
With my husband at my side I cherished in my breast
Longings for a tranquil life, a home of peace and rest.
Ah, a garden-bed I planted in his weary heart;
As its fairest ornament our love I hedged apart.
Flower and all have you uprooted with malignant hand;
In the dust it lies where thriving it did lately stand.

FURIA. Foolish weakling; you would guide the steps of Catiline?
Do you not perceive his heart was never wholly thine?
Think you that in such a soil your flower can survive?
In the sunny springtime only violets can thrive,
While the henbane grows in strength beneath a clouded grey;
And his soul was long ago a clouded autumn day.
All is lost to you. Soon dies the spark within his breast;
As a victim of revenge he shall go to his rest.

AURELIA. [With increasing vehemence.]
Thus he shall not perish; no, by all the gods of day!
To his weary heart my tears will somehow force a way.
If I find him pale and gory on the battlefield,
I shall throw my arms about him and his bosom shield,
Breathe upon his speechless lips the love within my soul,
Ease the pain within him and his suffering mind console.
Herald of revenge, your victim from you I shall wrest,
Bind him to the land of sunshine, to a home of rest;
If his eyes be dimmed already, stilled his beating heart,
Linked together arm in arm we shall this life depart.
Grant me, gods of mercy, in return for what I gave,
By the side of him I love, the stillness of the grave.

   [She goes.]

FURIA. [Gazes after her.]
Seek him, deluded soul; — I have no fear;
I hold the victory safe within my hands.

FURIA. The roar of battle grows; its rumble blends
With death-cries and the crash of broken shields.
Is he perchance now dying? Still alive?
Oh, blessed is this hour! The sinking moon
Secludes herself in massive thunderclouds.
One moment more it will be night anew
Ere comes the day; — and with the coming day
All will be over. In the dark he dies,
As in the dark he lived. O blessed hour!

[She listens.]

FURIA. Now sweeps the wind by, like an autumn gust,
And lapses slowly in the far-off distance.
The ponderous armies slowly sweep the plain.
Like angry ocean billows on they roll,
Unyielding, trampling down the fallen dead.
Out yonder I hear whines and moans and sighs, —
The final lullaby, — wherewith they lull
Themselves to rest and all their pallid brothers.
Now speaks the night-owl forth to welcome them
Into the kingdom of the gloomy shadows.

FURIA. [After a pause.]
How still it is. Now is he mine at last, —
Aye, mine alone, and mine forevermore.
Now we can journey toward the river Lethe —
And far beyond where never dawns the day.
Yet first I'll seek his bleeding body yonder,
And freely glut my eyes upon those features,
Hated and yet so fair, ere they be marred
By rising sunshine and by watchful vultures.

[She starts to go, but is suddenly startled at something.]

FURIA. What is that gliding o'er the meadow yonder?
Is it the misty vapors of the moor
That form a picture in the morning chill?

Now it draws near. — The shade of Catiline!
His spectre —! I can see his misty eye,
His broken shield, his sword bereft of blade.
Ah, he is surely dead; one thing alone, —
Remarkable, — his wound I do not see.

[CATILINE comes through the forest, pale and weary, with drooping head and troubled countenance.]

CATILINE. [To himself.] "Perish thou shalt by deed thine own,
And yet a stranger's hand shall fell thee."
Such was his prophecy. Now am I fallen —
Though struck by no one. Who will solve the riddle?

FURIA. I greet you after battle, Catiline!

CATILINE. Ah, who are you?

FURIA. I am a shadow's shadow.

CATILINE. You, Furia, — you it is! You welcome me?

FURIA. Welcome at last into our common home!
Now we can go — two shades — to Charon's bark.
Yet first — accept the wreath of victory.

[She picks some flowers, which she weaves into a wreath during the following.]

CATILINE. What make you there?

FURIA. Your brow I shall adorn.
But wherefore come you hither all alone?
A chieftain's ghost ten thousand dead should follow.
Then where are all your comrades, Catiline?

CATILINE. They slumber, Furia!

FURIA. Ah, they slumber still?

CATILINE. They slumber still, — and they will slumber long.
They slumber all. Steal softly through the forest,

Peer out across the plain,—disturb them not!
There will you find them in extended ranks.
They fell asleep lulled by the clang of steel;
They fell asleep,—and wakened not, as I did,
When in the distant hills the echoes died.
A shadow now you called me. True, I am
A shadow of myself. But do not think
Their slumber yonder is so undisturbed
And void of dreams. Oh, do not think so!

FURIA. Speak!
What may your comrades dream?

CATILINE. Ah, you shall hear.—
I led the battle with despairing heart,
And sought my death beneath the play of swords.
To right and left I saw my comrades fall;
Statilius first,—then one by one the rest;
My Curius fell trying to shield my breast;
All perished there beneath Rome's flaming sword,—
The sword that me alone passed by untouched.
Yes, Catiline was spared by the sword of Rome.
Half-stunned I stood there with my broken shield,
Aware of nothing as the waves of battle
Swept o'er me. I recovered first my senses
When all grew still again, and I looked up
And saw the struggle seething—far behind me!
How long I stood there? Only this I know,—
I stood alone among my fallen comrades.
But there was life within those misty eyes;
The corners of their mouths betrayed a smile;
And they addressed their smile and gaze to me,
Who stood alone erect among the dead,—
Who had for ages fought for them and Rome,—
Who stood there lonely and disgraced, untouched
By Roman sword. Then perished Catiline.

FURIA. False have you read your fallen comrades' dreams;
False have you judged the reason of your fall.
Their smiles and glances were but invitations
To sleep with them —

CATILINE. Yes, if I only could!

FURIA. Have courage, — spectre of a former hero;
Your hour of rest is near. Come, bend your head; —
I shall adorn you with the victor's crown.

[She offers the wreath to him.]

CATILINE. Bah, — what is that? A poppy-wreath —!

FURIA. [With wild glee.] Well, yes;
Are not such poppies pretty? They will glow
Around your forehead like a fringe of blood.

CATILINE. No, cast the wreath away! I hate this crimson.

FURIA. [Laughs aloud.]
Ah, you prefer the pale and feeble shades?
Good! I shall bring the garland of green rushes
That Sylvia carried in her dripping locks,
The day she came afloat upon the Tiber?

CATILINE. Alas, what visions —!

FURIA. Shall I bring you rather
The thorny brambles from the market-place,
With crimson-spots, the stain of civic blood,
That flowed at your behest, my Catiline?

CATILINE. Enough!

FURIA. Or would you like a crown of leaves
From the old winter oak near mother's home,
That withered when a young dishonored woman

With piercing cries distraught leaped in the river?

CATILINE. Pour out at once your measures of revenge
Upon my head —

FURIA. I am your very eye, —
Your very memory, your very doom.

CATILINE. But wherefore now?

FURIA. His goal at length attained,
The traveller spent looks back from whence he came.

CATILINE. Have I then reached my goal? Is this the goal?
I am no longer living, — nor yet buried.
Where lies the goal?

FURIA. In sight, — if you but will.

CATILINE. A will I have no longer; my will perished
When all the things I willed once, came to naught.

CATILINE. [Waves his arms.]
Away, — away from me, ye sallow shades!
What claim you here of me, ye men and women?
I cannot give you —! Oh, this multitude —!

FURIA. To earth your spirit still is closely bound!
These thousand-threaded nets asunder tear!
Come, let me press this wreath upon your locks, —
'Tis gifted with a strong and soothing virtue;
It kills the memory, lulls the soul to rest!

CATILINE. [Huskily.]
It kills the memory? Dare I trust your word?

Then press your poison-wreath upon my forehead.

FURIA. [Puts the wreath on his head.]
Now it is yours! Thus decked you shall appear
Before the prince of darkness, Catiline!

CATILINE. Away! away! I yearn to go below; —
I long to pass into the spirit lands.
Let us together go! What holds me here?
What stays my steps? Behind me here I feel
Upon the morning sky a misty star; —
It holds me in the land of living men;
It draws me as the moon attracts the sea.

    FURIA. Away! Away!

CATILINE. It beckons and it twinkles.
I cannot follow you until this light
Is quenched entirely, or by clouds obscured, —
I see it clearly now; 'tis not a star;
It is a human heart, throbbing and warm;
It binds me here; it fascinates and draws me
As draws the evening star the eye of children.

    FURIA. Then stop this beating heart!

    CATILINE. What do you mean?

FURIA. The dagger in your belt — . A single thrust, —
The star will vanish and the heart will die
That stand between us like an enemy.

    CATILINE. Ah, I should — ? Sharp and shining is the dagger —

CATILINE. [With a cry.]
Aurelia! O Aurelia, where — where are you?
Were you but here — ! No, no, — I will not see you!
And yet methinks all would be well again,
And peace would come, if I could lay my head

Upon your bosom and repent — repent!

FURIA. And what would you repent?

CATILINE. Oh, everything!
That I have been, that I have ever lived.

FURIA. 'Tis now too late — too late! Whence now you stand
No path leads back again. — Go try it, fool!
Now am I going home. Place you your head
Upon her breast and see if there you find
The blessed peace your weary soul desires.

FURIA. [With increasing wildness.]
Soon will the thousand dead rise up again;
Dishonored women will their numbers join;
And all, — aye, they will all demand of you
The life, the blood, the honor you destroyed.
In terror you will flee into the night, —
Will roam about the earth on every strand,
Like old Actean, hounded by his dogs, —
A shadow hounded by a thousand shades!

CATILINE. I see it, Furia. Here I have no peace.
I am an exile in the world of light!
I'll go with you into the spirit realms; —
The bond that binds me I will tear asunder.

FURIA. Why grope you with the dagger?

CATILINE. She shall die.

[The lightning strikes and the thunder rolls.]

FURIA. The mighty powers rejoice at your resolve! —
See, Catiline, — see, yonder comes your wife.

[AURELIA comes through the forest in an anxious search.]

AURELIA. Where shall I find him? Where — where can he be!
I've searched in vain among the dead —

[Discovers him.]

AURELIA. Great heavens, —
My Catiline!

[She rushes toward him.]

CATILINE. [Bewildered.] Speak not that name again!

AURELIA. You are alive?

[Is about to throw herself in his arms.]

CATILINE. [Thrusting her aside.] Away! I'm not alive.

AURELIA. Oh, hear me, dearest — !

CATILINE. No, I will not hear!
I hate you. I see through your cunning wiles.
You wish to chain me to a living death.
Cease staring at me! Ah, your eyes torment me, —
They pierce like daggers through my very soul!
Ah, yes, the dagger! Die! Come, close your eyes —

[He draws the dagger and seizes her by the hand.]

AURELIA. Keep guard, oh gracious gods, o'er him and me!

CATILINE. Quick, close your eyes; close them, I say; — in them
I see the starlight and the morning sky — .
Now shall I quench the heavenly star of dawn!

[The thunder rolls again.]

CATILINE. Your heart; your blood! Now speak the gods of life
Their last farewell to you and Catiline!

[He lifts the dagger toward her bosom; she escapes into the tent;
he pursues her.]

FURIA. [Listens.] She stretches out her hand imploringly.
She pleads with him for life. He hears her not.
He strikes her down! She reels in her own blood!

[CATILINE comes slowly out of the tent with the dagger in his hand.]

CATILINE. Now am I free. Soon I shall cease to be.
Now sinks my soul in vague oblivion.
My eyes are growing dim, my hearing faint,
As if through rushing waters. Ah, do you know
What I have slain with this my little dagger?
Not her alone, — but all the hearts on earth, —
All living things, all things that grow and bloom; —
The starlight have I dimmed, the crescent moon,
The flaming sun. Ah, see, — it fails to rise;
'Twill never rise again; the sun is dead.
Now is the whole wide realm of earth transformed
Into a huge and clammy sepulchre,
Its vault of leaden grey; — beneath this vault
Stand you and I, bereft of light and darkness,
Of death and life, — two restless exiled shadows.

FURIA. Now stand we, Catiline, before our goal!

CATILINE. No, one step more — before I reach my goal.
Relieve me of my burden! Do you not see,
I bend beneath the corpse of Catiline?
A dagger through the corpse of Catiline!

[He shows her the dagger.]

CATILINE. Come, Furia, set me free! Come, take this dagger; —
On it the star of morning I impaled; —
Take it — and plunge it straightway through the corpse;
Then it will loose its hold, and I am free.

FURIA. [Takes the dagger.]
Your will be done, whom I have loved in hate!
Shake off your dust and come with me to rest.

[She buries the dagger deep in his heart; he sinks down at the foot
of the tree.]

CATILINE. [After a moment comes to consciousness
again, passes his hand across his forehead, and speaks
faintly.] Now, mysterious voice, your prophecy I understand!
I shall perish by my own, yet by a stranger's hand.
Nemesis has wrought her end. Shroud me, gloom of night!
Raise your billows, murky Styx, roll on in all your might!
Ferry me across in safety; speed the vessel on
Toward the silent prince's realm, the land of shadows wan.
Two roads there are running yonder; I shall journey dumb
Toward the left—

AURELIA. [From the tent, pale and faltering, her bosom bloody.]
—no, toward the right! Oh, toward Elysium!

CATILINE. [Startled.]
How this bright and lurid picture fills my soul with dread!
She herself it is! Aurelia, speak,—are you not dead?

AURELIA. [Kneels before him.]
No, I live that I may still your agonizing cry,—
Live that I may lean my bosom on your breast and die.

CATILINE. Oh, you live!

AURELIA. I did but swoon; though my two eyes grew blurred,
Dimly yet I followed you and heard your every word.
And my love a spouse's strength again unto me gave;—
Breast to breast, my Catiline, we go into the grave!

CATILINE. Oh, how gladly would I go! Yet all in vain you sigh.
We must part. Revenge compels me with a hollow cry.

You can hasten, free and blithesome, forth to peace and light;
I must cross the river Lethe down into the night.

[The day dawns in the background.]

AURELIA. [Points toward the increasing light.]
No, the terrors and the gloom of death love scatters far.
See, the storm-clouds vanish; faintly gleams the morning star.

AURELIA. [With uplifted arms.]
Light is victor! Grand and full of freshness dawns the day!
Follow me, then! Death already speeds me on his way.

[She sinks down over him.]

CATILINE. [Presses her to himself and speaks with his last
strength.] Oh, how sweet! Now I remember my forgotten dream,
How the darkness was dispersed before a radiant beam,
How the song of children ushered in the new-born day.
Ah, my eye grows dim, my strength is fading fast away;
But my mind is clearer now than ever it has been:
All the wanderings of my life loom plainly up within.
Yes, my life a tempest was beneath the lightning blaze;
But my death is like the morning's rosy-tinted haze.

[Bends over her.]

CATILINE.
You have driven the gloom away; peace dwells within my breast.
I shall seek with you the dwelling place of light and rest!

CATILINE. [He tears the dagger quickly out of his breast and
speaks with dying voice.]
The gods of dawn are smiling in atonement from above;
All the powers of darkness you have conquered with your love!

[During the last scene FURIA has withdrawn farther and farther into the background and disappears at last among the trees. CATI-LINE's head sinks down on AURELIA's breast; they die.]

* * * * *

THE WARRIOR'S BARROW

[Kaempehojen]

A Dramatic Poem in One Act

1854

* * * * *

DRAMATIS PERSONÆ

RODERIK An old recluse.

BLANKA His foster-daughter.

GANDALF A sea-king from Norway.

ASGAUT An old viking.

HROLLOUG " " "

JOSTEJN " " "

Several VIKINGS

HEMMING A young scald in Gandalf's service.

* * * * *

SETTING

The action takes place on a small island off the coast of Sicily shortly before the introduction of Christianity into Norway.

An open place surrounded by trees near the shore. To the left in the background the ruins of an old temple. In the center of the scene a huge barrow upon which is a monument decked with flower wreaths.

* * * * *

SCENE I

[At the right of the stage sits RODERIK writing. To the left BLANKA in a half reclining position.]

BLANKA. Lo! the sky in dying glory
  Surges like a sea ablaze, —
  It is all so still before me,
  Still as in a sylvan maze.
  Summer evening's mellow power
  Settles round us like a dove,
  Hovers like a swan above
  Ocean wave and forest flower.
  In the orange thicket slumber
  Gods and goddesses of yore,
  Stone reminders in great number
  Of a world that is no more.
  Virtue, valor, trust are gone,
  Rich in memory alone;
  Could there be a more complete
  Picture of the South effete?

[Rises.]

BLANKA. But my father has related
  Stories of a distant land,
  Of a life, fresh, unabated,
  Neither carved nor wrought by hand!
  Here the spirit has forever
  Vanished into stone and wave, —
  There it breathes as free as ever,
  Like a warrior strong and brave!
  When the evening's crystallizing
  Vapors settle on my breast,
  Lo! I see before me rising
  Norway's snow-illumined crest!
  Here is life decayed and dying,
  Sunk in torpor, still, forlorn, —
  There go avalanches flying,
  Life anew in death is born!

If I had the white swan's coat —

RODERIK. [After a pause writing.]
"Then, it is said, will Ragnarök have stilled
The wilder powers, brought forth a chastened life;
All-Father, Balder, and the gentle Freya
Will rule again the race of man in peace!" —

[After having watched her for a moment.]

RODERIK. But, Blanka, now you dream away again;
You stare through space completely lost in thought, —
What is it that you seek?

BLANKA. [Draws near.] Forgive me, father!
I merely followed for a space the swan,
That sailed on snowy wings across the sea.

RODERIK. And if I had not stopped you in your flight,
My young and pretty little swan! who knows
How far you might have flown away from me, —
Perchance to Thule?

BLANKA. And indeed why not?
To Thule flies the swan in early spring,
If only to return again each fall.

[Seats herself at his feet.]

BLANKA. Yet I — I am no swan, — no, call me rather
A captured falcon, sitting tame and true,
A golden ring about his foot.

RODERIK. Well, — and the ring?

BLANKA. The ring? That is my love for you, dear father!
With that you have your youthful falcon bound,

I cannot fly, — not even though I wished to.

[Rises.]

BLANKA. But when I see the swan sail o'er the wave,
Light as a cloud before the summer wind,
Then I remember all that you have told
Of the heroic life in distant Thule;
Then, as it seems, the bird is like a bark
With dragon head and wings of burnished gold;
I see the youthful hero in the prow,
A copper helmet on his yellow locks,
With eyes of blue, a manly, heaving breast,
His sword held firmly in his mighty hand.
I follow him upon his rapid course,
And all my dreams run riot round his bark,
And frolic sportively like merry dolphins
In fancy's deep and cooling sea!

RODERIK. O you, —
You are an ardent dreamer, my good child, —
I almost fear your thoughts too often dwell
Upon the people in the rugged North.

BLANKA. And, father, whose the fault, if it were so?

RODERIK. You mean that I — ?

BLANKA. Yes, what else could I mean;
You live yourself but in the memory
Of early days among these mighty Norsemen;
Do not deny that often as you speak
Of warlike forays, combats, fights,
Your cheek begins to flush, your eye to glow;
It seems to me that you grow young again.

RODERIK. Yes, yes, but I have reason so to do;
For I have lived among them in the North,

114

And every bit that memory calls to mind
Is like a page to me from my own saga.
But you, however, fostered in the South,
Who never saw the silver-tinted mountains,
Who never heard the trumpet's echoing song, —
Ah, how could you be moved by what I tell?

BLANKA. Oh, must a human being see and hear
All things but with his outer senses then?
Has not the inner soul, too, eye and ear,
With which it can both see and hearken well?
'Tis true it is with eyes of flesh I see
The richly glowing color of the rose;
But with the spirit's eye I see within
A lovely elf, a fairy butterfly,
Who archly hides behind the crimson leaves,
And singeth of a secret power from heaven
That gave the flower brightness and perfume.

   RODERIK. True, true, my child!

BLANKA. I almost do believe
That just because I do not really see,
The whole looms up more beautiful in thought;
That, father, is the way with you at least!
The ancient sagas and heroic lays, —
These you remember, speak of with delight,
And scratch in runic script upon your parchment;
But if I ask about your youthful life
In Norway's distant realm, your eyes grow dark,
Your lips are silent, and it seems at times
Your bosom houses gloomy memories.

RODERIK. [Rises.]
Come, speak no more, good child, about the past.
Who is there then whose youthful memories
Are altogether free from self-reproach;

You know, the Norsemen are a savage lot.

BLANKA. But are the warriors of the South less fierce?
Have you forgot that night, now ten years past,
The time the strangers landed on the coast,
And plundered —?

RODERIK. [Visibly ill at ease.] Say no more now, — let us hence;
The sundown soon will be upon us; — come!

BLANKA. [As they go.] Give me your hand!

[Stops.]

BLANKA. No, wait!

RODERIK. What is the matter?

BLANKA. I have today for the first time forgot —

RODERIK. And what have you forgot?

BLANKA. [Points to the barrow.] Behold the wreath!

RODERIK. It is —

BLANKA. The withered one of yesterday;
I have forgot today to make the change;
Yet, let me take you to the cabin first,
Then shall I venture out in search of flowers;
The violet never is so sweet and rare
As when the dew has bathed its silver lining;
The budding rose is never quite so fair
As when 'tis plucked in child-like sleep reclining!

[They go out at the back to the right.]

* * * * *

SCENE II

[GANDALF and the VIKINGS enter from the right.]

ASGAUT. Now we shall soon be there.

GANDALF. Point out the place!

ASGAUT. No, wait till we have gone beyond the wood.
There was still standing on the rocky cliff
Against the sea a remnant of the wall, —
I dare say it is standing there to-day.

JOSTEJN. But tell us, king, what can it profit us
To tramp about here on the isle like fools?

HROLLOUG. Yes, tell us what shall —

GANDALF. You shall hold your tongues!
And blindly follow where your king commands!

GANDALF. [To ASGAUT.]
It seems to me, however, you cleaned house
Too well when you were last here on the isle;
You might have left a little, I should think,
For me and my revenge!

HROLLOUG. You are the king,
And loyalty we pledged you at the thing,
But when we followed you upon the war path,
It was to win our share of fame and glory.

JOSTEJN. And golden treasures, Hrolloug, golden treasures.

SEVERAL. That, Gandalf, is the law, and heed it well!

GANDALF. I know the law perhaps as well as you;
But is there not since days of old a law
And covenant with us that when a kinsman
Falls slain before the enemy and his corpse

Unburied lies a prey unto the raven,
Blood vengeance must be had?

SOME. Yes, so it is!

GANDALF. Then stand you ready with your sword and shield, —
You have a king to avenge and I a father!

[Commotion among the VIKINGS.]

JOSTEJN. A king?

HROLLOUG. A father?

GANDALF. Wait, — I shall relate
How all this stands. You know, my father was
A mighty viking. Twelve years gone it is
Since he the last time sallied forth one spring
With Asgaut there and all his old time warriors.
Two years he roamed about from strand to strand,
Visiting Bratland, Valland, even Blaaland;
At length he went and harried Sicily,
And there heard stories of a wealthy chief,
Who lived upon this island in a castle
With sturdy walls built on a rocky base,
And in it there were costly treasures hid.
At night he took his men and went ashore,
And razed the castle walls with fire and sword.
Himself went foremost like an angry bear,
And in the fury of the fight saw not
How all his warriors fell about him dead;
And when the morning sun rose in the east,
There lay the castle smouldering in ruin.
Asgaut alone survived with one or two, —
My father and the hundred others there
Had ridden to Valhalla through the flames.

ASGAUT. I hoisted every sail upon the bark,
And turned the prow straight homeward to the North;
There sought I all in vain for Gandalf king;

The youthful eagle, I was told, had flown
Across the sea to Iceland or the Faroes.
I hastened after him but found no trace,-
Yet everywhere I went his name was known;
For though his bark sped cloud-like in the storm,
Yet flew his fame on even swifter wings.
At last this spring I found him, as you know;
It was in Italy; I told him then
What things had happened, how his father died,
And Gandalf swore by all Valhalla's gods
Blood-vengeance he would take with fire and sword.

JOSTEJN. It is an ancient law and should be honored!
But had I been in your place, Gandalf king,
I should have lingered on in Italy, —
For there was gold to win.

HROLLOUG. And honor too.

GANDALF. That is your loyalty to your dead king.

JOSTEJN. Come, come now; no offence; I merely meant
The dead could wait perhaps.

ASGAUT. [With suppressed rage.] You paltry race!

JOSTEJN. But now that we are here —

HROLLOUG. Yes; let us raise
Unto the king a worthy monument!

SOME. Yes, yes!

OTHERS. With bloodshed and with fire!

ASGAUT. Now that I like!

GANDALF. And now away to spy around the island;
For even tonight blood-vengeance shall be mine;
If not, I must myself fall.

ASGAUT. So he swore.

GANDALF. I swore it solemnly by all the gods!
And once again I swear it —

HEMMING. [With a harp on his shoulder has during the preceding emerged from among the WARRIORS and cries out imploringly.] Swear not, Gandalf!

GANDALF. What troubles you?

HEMMING. Swear not here in this wood!
Here in the South our gods can never hear;
Out on your bark, up North among the hills,
There they still hearken to you, but not here!

ASGAUT. Have you too breathed the poison of the South?

HEMMING. In Italy I heard the pious monks
Tell lovely stories of the holy Christ,
And what they told still lingers in my mind
Through night and day and will no more be gone.

GANDALF. I had you brought with me because in youth
You showed great promise of poetic gifts.
You were to see my bold and warlike deeds,
So that when I, King Gandalf, old and gray,
Sat with my warriors round the oaken table,
The king's young scald might while away
Long winter evenings with heroic lays,
And sing at last a saga of my deeds;
The hero's fame voiced in the poet's song
Outlives the monument upon his grave.
But now, be off, and if you choose go cast
Your harp aside and don the monkish cowl.
Aha! King Gandalf has a mighty scald!

[The VIKINGS go into the forest to the left; HEMMING follows them.]

ASGAUT. It is a mouldy time we live in now;
Our faith and customs from the olden days
Are everywhere upon the downward path.
Lucky it is that I am growing old;
My eyes shall never see the North decay.
But you, King Gandalf, you are young and strong;
And wheresoe'er you roam in distant lands,
Remember that it is a royal task
To guard the people and defend the gods!

   [He follows the rest.]

GANDALF. [After a pause.] Hm, he has no great confidence in me.
'Tis well he went! Whenever he is near,
It is as if a burden weighed me down.
The grim old viking with his rugged face, —
He looks like Asathor, who with his belt
Of strength and Mjölnir stood within the grove,
Carved out in marble, near my father's home.
My father's home! Who knows, alas! how things
Around the ancient landmarks now may look! —
Mountains and fields are doubtless still the same;
The people — ? Have they still the same old heart?
No, there is fallen mildew o'er the age,
And it is that which saps the Northern life
And eats away like poison what is best.
Well, I will homeward, — save what still is left
To save before it falls to utter ruin.

GANDALF. [After a pause during which he looks around.]
How lovely in these Southern groves it is;
My pine groves can not boast such sweet perfume.

   [He perceives the mound.]

GANDALF. What now? A warrior's grave? No doubt it hides
A countryman from those more stirring days.
A warrior's barrow in the South! — 'Tis only just;

It was the South gave us our mortal wound.
How lovely it is here! It brings to mind
One winter night when as a lad I sat
Upon my father's knee before the hearth,
The while he told me stories of the gods,
Of Odin, Balder, and the mighty Thor;
And when I mentioned Freya's grove to him,
He pictured it exactly like this grove, —
But when I asked him something more of Freya,
What she herself was like, the old man laughed
And answered as he placed me on my feet,
"A woman will in due time tell you that!"

GANDALF. [Listening.]
Hush! Footsteps in the forest! Quiet, Gandalf,-
They bring the first fruits of your blood-revenge!

[He steps aside so that he is half concealed among the bushes to
the right.]

* * * * *

SCENE III

[GANDALF. BLANKA with oak leaves in her hair and a basket of
flowers enters from the left.]

BLANKA. [Seated at the left busily weaving a flower wreath.]
Fountains may murmur in the sunny vales,
Resplendent billows roll beneath the shore;
Nor fountain's murmur, nor the billow's song
Has half the magic of those flowers there,
That stand in clusters round the barrow's edge
And nod at one another lovingly;
They draw me hither during night and day, —
And it is here I long to come and dream.
The wreath is done. The hero's monument,

So hard and cold, shall under it be hid.
Yes, it is beautiful!

[Pointing to the mound.]

BLANKA. A vanished life,
Of giant strength, lies mouldering in the ground, —
And the memorial which should speak to men, —
A cold unyielding stone like yonder one!
But then comes art, and with a friendly hand
She gathers flowers from the breast of nature
And hides the ugly, unresponsive stone
With snow-white lilies, sweet forget-me-nots.

[She ascends the barrow, hangs the wreath over the monument,
and speaks after a pause.]

BLANKA. Again my dreams go sailing to the North
Like birds of passage o'er the ocean waves;
I feel an urging where I long to go,
And willingly I heed the secret power,
Which has its royal seat within the soul.
I stand in Norway, am a hero's bride,
And from the mountain peak watch eagle-like.
O'er shining waves the vessel heaves in sight. —
Oh, like the gull fly to your fatherland!
I am a Southern child, I cannot wait;
I tear the oaken wreath out of my hair, —
Take this, my hero! 'Tis the second message
I greet you with, — my yearning was the first.

[She throws the wreath. GANDALF steps forth and seizes it.]

BLANKA. What's this? There stands a —

[She rubs her eyes and stares amazed at him.]

No, it is no dream.
Who are you, stranger? What is it you seek

Here on the shore?

GANDALF. Step first from off the mound, —
Then we can talk at ease.

BLANKA. [Comes down.] Well, here I am!

BLANKA. [Aside as she looks him over.]
The chain mail o'er his breast, the copper helmet, —
Exactly as my father has related.

BLANKA. [Aloud.] Take off your helmet!

GANDALF. Why?

BLANKA. Well, take it off!

BLANKA. [Aside.]
Two sparkling eyes, locks like a field of grain, —
Exactly as I saw him in my dream.

GANDALF. Who are you, woman?

BLANKA. I? A poor, poor child!

GANDALF. Yet certainly the fairest on the isle.

BLANKA. The fairest? That indeed is possible,
For here there's no one else.

GANDALF. What, — no one else?

BLANKA. Unless my father be, — but he is old
And has a silver beard, as long as this;
No, after all I think I win the prize.

GANDALF. You have a merry spirit.

BLANKA. Not always now!

GANDALF. But tell me, pray, how this is possible;
You say you live alone here with your father,

Yet I have heard men say most certainly
The island here is thickly populated?

BLANKA. It was so once, three years ago or more;
But, — well, it is a sad and mournful tale —
Yet you shall hear it if you wish.

GANDALF. Yes, certainly!

BLANKA. You see, three years ago —

[Seats herself.]

BLANKA. Come, seat yourself!

GANDALF. [Steps back a pace.] No, sit you down, I'll stand.

BLANKA. Three years ago there came, God knows from whence,
A warlike band of robbers to the isle;
They plundered madly as they went about,
And murdered everything they found alive.
A few escaped as best they could by flight
And sought protection in my father's castle,
Which stood upon the cliff right near the sea.

GANDALF. Your father's, did you say?

BLANKA. My father's, yes. —
It was a cloudy evening when they burst
Upon the castle gate, tore through the wall,
Rushed in the court, and murdered right and left.
I fled into the darkness terrified,
And sought a place of refuge in the forest.
I saw our home go whirling up in flames,
I heard the clang of shields, the cries of death. —
Then everything grew still; for all were dead. —
The savage band proceeded to the shore
And sailed away. — I sat upon the cliff
The morning after, near the smouldering ruins.
I was the only one whom they had spared.

GANDALF. But you just told me that your father lives.

BLANKA. My foster-father; wait, and you shall hear!
I sat upon the cliff oppressed and sad,
And listened to the awful stillness round;
There issued forth a faint and feeble cry,
As from beneath the rocky cleft beneath my feet;
I listened full of fear, then went below,
And found a stranger, pale with loss of blood.
I ventured nearer, frightened as I was,
Bound up his wounds and tended him, —

GANDALF. And he?

BLANKA. Told me as he recovered from his wounds,
That he had come aboard a merchantman,
Had reached the island on the very day
The castle was destroyed, — took refuge there
And fought the robber band with all his might
Until he fell, faint with the loss of blood,
Into the rocky cleft wherein I found him.
And ever since we two have lived together;
He built for us a cabin in the wood,
I grew to love him more than any one.
But you must see him, — come!

GANDALF. No, wait, — not now!
We meet in ample time, I have no doubt.

BLANKA. Well, all right, as you please; but rest assured
He would be glad to greet you 'neath his roof;
For you must know that hospitality
Is found not only in the North.

GANDALF. The North?
You know then —

BLANKA. Whence you come, you mean? Oh, yes!
My father has so often told of you
That I the moment that I saw you —

GANDALF. Yet you
Were not afraid!

   BLANKA. Afraid? And why afraid?

   GANDALF. Has he not told you then, — of course if not —

BLANKA. Told me that you were fearless heroes? Yes!
But pray, why should that frighten me?
I know you seek your fame on distant shores,
In manly combat with all doughty warriors;
But I have neither sword nor coat of mail,
Then why should I fear —

GANDALF. No, of course, of course!
But still, those strangers who destroyed the castle?

   BLANKA. And what of them?

GANDALF. Only, — has not your father
Told you from whence they came?

BLANKA. Never! How could he!
Strangers they were alike to him and us.
But if you wish I'll ask him right away.

   GANDALF. [Quickly.] No, let it be.

BLANKA. Ah, now I understand!
You wish to know where you can seek them now,
And take blood-vengeance, as you call it.

GANDALF. Ah,
Blood-vengeance! Thanks! The word I had forgot;

You bring me back —

BLANKA. But do you know, it is
An ugly practice.

    GANDALF. [Going toward the background.] Farewell!

    BLANKA. O, you are going?

    GANDALF. We meet in time.

    [Stops.]

GANDALF. Tell me this one thing more:
What warrior is it rests beneath the mound?

    BLANKA. I do not know.

GANDALF. You do not know, and still
You scatter flowers on the hero's grave.

BLANKA. My father led me here one morning early
And pointed out to me the fresh-made mound,
Which I had never seen upon the strand.
He bade me say my morning prayers out here,
And in my supplications to remember
Those who had harried us with sword and fire.

    GANDALF. And you?

BLANKA. Each morning from that day to this
I sent a prayer to heaven for their salvation;
And every evening flowers afresh I wove
Into a garland for the grave.

GANDALF. Yes, strange!
How can you pray thus for your enemy?

    BLANKA. My faith commands me.

GANDALF. [Vehemently.] Such a faith is craven;
It is the faith which saps the hero's strength;
'Twas therefore that the great, heroic life
Died feebly in the South!

BLANKA. But now suppose
My craven faith, as you see fit to call it,
Could be transplanted to your virgin soil, —
I know full well, there would spring forth a mass
Of flowers so luxuriant as to hide
The naked mountain.

GANDALF. Let the mountain stand
In nakedness until the end of time!

   BLANKA. O! Take me with you!

GANDALF. What do you mean?
I sail for home —

BLANKA. Well, I shall sail with you;
For I have often traveled in my dreams
To far-off Norway, where you live mid snow
And ice and sombre woods of towering pines.
There should come mirth and laughter in the hall,
If I could have my say, I promise you;
For I am merry; — have you any scald?

GANDALF. I had one, but the sultry Southern air
Has loosened all the strings upon his harp, —
They sing no longer —

BLANKA. Good! Then shall I be
Your scald.

GANDALF. And you? — You could go with us there,
And leave your father and your home?

BLANKA. [Laughing.] Aha!
You think I meant it seriously?

GANDALF. Was it
Only a jest?

BLANKA. Alas! a foolish dream
I often used to dream before we met, —
Which often I no doubt shall dream again,
When you —

   [Suddenly breaking off.]

   BLANKA. You stare so fixedly.

   GANDALF. Do I?

   BLANKA. Why, yes! What are you thinking of?

   GANDALF. I? Nothing!

   BLANKA. Nothing?

GANDALF. That is, I scarcely know myself;
And yet I do — and you shall hear it now:
I thought of you and how you would transplant
Your flowers in the North, when suddenly
My own faith came as if by chance to mind.
One word therein I never understood
Before; now have you taught me what it means.

   BLANKA. And that is what?

GANDALF. Valfader, it is said,
Receives but half the warriors slain in battle;
The other half to Freya goes by right.
That I could never fully comprehend;

But—now I understand,—I am myself
A fallen warrior, and to Freya goes
The better part of me.

   BLANKA. [Amazed.] What does this mean?

   GANDALF. Well, in a word, then know—

BLANKA. [Quickly.] No, say it not!
I dare not tarry longer here to-night,—
My father waits, and I must go; farewell!

   GANDALF. O, you are going?

BLANKA. [Takes the wreath of oak leaves which he has
let fall and throws it around his helmet.] You can keep it now.
Lo, what I hitherto bestowed on you
In dreams, I grant you now awake.

   GANDALF. Farewell!

   [He goes quickly out to the right.]

   * * * * *

SCENE IV

BLANKA. [Alone.]
  He is gone! Ah, perfect stillness
  Rules upon the barren strand.
  Perfect stillness, grave-like stillness
  Rules my heart with heavy hand.
  Came he then to vanish only
  Through the mist, a ray of light?
  Soon he flies, a sea-gull lonely,
  Far away into the night!
  What is left me of this lover?
  But a flower in the dark:
  In my loneliness to hover

Like a petrel round his bark!

[The war trumpet of the Vikings is heard from the left.]
BLANKA. Ah! What was that! A trumpet from the wood!
* * * * *

SCENE V

[BLANKA, GANDALF from the right.]

GANDALF. [Aside.] It is too late!

BLANKA. O, there he is again!
What do you want?

GANDALF. Quick, — quick, away from here!

BLANKA. What do you mean?

GANDALF. Away! There's danger here!

BLANKA. What danger?

GANDALF. Death!

BLANKA. I do not understand you.

GANDALF. I thought to hide it from you, — hence I went
To call my people to the ship again
And sail away; you never should have known, —
The trumpet warns me that it is too late, —
That they are coming.

BLANKA. Who are coming?

GANDALF. Then know, —
The strangers who once harried on the isle
Were vikings like myself.

BLANKA. From Norway?

GANDALF. Yes.
My father, who was chief among them, fell, —
Hence must he be avenged.

BLANKA. Avenged?

GANDALF. Such is
The custom.

BLANKA. Ah, I see now!

GANDALF. Here they come!
Stand close behind me!

BLANKA. Man of blood, — away!

* * * * *

SCENE VI

[The Preceding.]

[ASGAUT, HEMMING and the VIKINGS, who lead RODERIK between them.]

ASGAUT. [To GANDALF.] A meagre find, yet something, to be sure.

BLANKA. My father!

[She throws herself in his arms.]

RODERIK. Blanka! O, my child!

JOSTEJN. A woman!
He will have company.

ASGAUT. Yes, straight to Hell!

BLANKA. O father, wherefore have you never told me —

RODERIK. Hush! Hush! my child!

[Points to GANDALF.]

RODERIK. Is this your chieftain?

ASGAUT. Yes.

ASGAUT. [To GANDALF.]
This man can tell you how your father died;
For he was in the thick of it, he says,
The only one to get away alive.

GANDALF. Hush! I will nothing hear.

ASGAUT. Good; let us then
Begin the task.

BLANKA. O God! what will they do?

GANDALF. [In an undertone.] I cannot, Asgaut!

ASGAUT. [Likewise.] Is our king afraid?
Has woman's flattering tongue beguiled his mind?

GANDALF. No matter, — I have said —

ASGAUT. Bethink yourself, —
Your standing with your warriors is at stake.
Your word you pledged Valhalla's mighty gods,
And if you fail a dastard you'll be judged.
Do not forget our faith is insecure —
And wavering; one blow can strike its root,
And if the blow comes from the king above,
It will have had a mortal wound.

GANDALF. Ah me!
That was a most unhappy oath I swore.

ASGAUT. [To the VIKINGS.] Now ready, warriors!

BLANKA. Will you murder him,
An old, defenseless man?

ASGAUT. Down with them both!

BLANKA. O God!

HROLLOUG. The woman is too fair! Let her
Return with us.

JOSTEJN. [Laughing.] Yes, as a warrior maid.

GANDALF. Stand back!

RODERIK. O spare, — O spare at least my child!
The slayer of your chieftain I will bring you,
If you will only spare her!

GANDALF. [Quickly.] Bring him here,
And she is free. What say you?

THE VIKINGS. She is free!

BLANKA. [To RODERIK.] You promise that?

ASGAUT. Then fetch him!

RODERIK. Here he stands!

SOME. Ha, that old man!

GANDALF. O woe!

BLANKA. No, no, you shall not —

RODERIK. Struck by this hand the viking found his death,
Now rests he peacefully in yonder mound!

GANDALF. My father's barrow!

RODERIK. He was strong and brave;
Wherefore I laid him here in viking style.

GANDALF. Since he is buried, then, —

ASGAUT. Though he be buried,
The fallen king cries for revenge, — strike, strike!

BLANKA. He is deceiving you!

BLANKA. [To GANDALF.] Do you not see
It is alone his daughter he would save?
Yet, how should your kind understand a soul
That sacrifices all —

GANDALF. I do not understand?
You do not think I can?

GANDALF. [To the VIKINGS.] He shall not die!

ASGAUT. How so?

BLANKA. O father! He is good like you.

ASGAUT. You mean to break your oath?

GANDALF. No, I shall keep it!

JOSTEJN. Then what have you in mind?

HROLLOUG. Explain!

GANDALF. I swore
To take revenge or else to die myself.
Well, he is free, — I to Valhalla go.

BLANKA. [To RODERIK.] What does he mean?

ASGAUT. Your honor you would save? —

GANDALF. Go, — hold a ship in readiness for me,
With hoisted sail, the pyre light in the prow;
In ancient fashion I shall go aboard!
Behold, the evening breeze blows from the strand, —
On crimson wings I sail into Valhalla!

[JOSTEJN goes out to the right.]

ASGAUT. Ah, 'tis the woman who has cast her spell on you!

BLANKA. No, you must live!

GANDALF. I live? No, to the gods
I must be true, I cannot break with them.

BLANKA. Your oath is bloody, Balder hates it.

GANDALF. Yes,
But Balder lives no longer with us now!

BLANKA. For you he lives; your soul is gentleness.

GANDALF. Yes, to my ruin! It became my task
As king to keep intact our great ideal, —
But I lack strength enough! Come, Asgaut, you
Shall take the kingly sceptre from my hand;
You are a warrior of the truest steel;
On me the Southern plague has been at work.
But if I cannot for my people live,
I now can die for them.

ASGAUT. Well said, King Gandalf!

BLANKA. Then need no more be said! Die like a hero,
Faithful and true unto the very end!
But now that we must part forever, — know,
That when you die yourself to keep your oath
You are then likewise marking me for death!

GANDALF. What! You for death?

BLANKA. My life was like a flower,
Transplanted in an unfamiliar soil,
Which therefore slumbered in its prison folds:
Then came a sunbeam from the distant home, —
O, that was you, my Gandalf! Opened then
The flower its calyx. In another hour,

Alas! the sunbeam paled, — the flower died!

GANDALF. O, have I understood you right? You could?
Then is my promise thrice unfortunate!

BLANKA. But we shall meet again!

GANDALF. O, nevermore!
You go to heaven and the holy Christ,
I to Valhalla; silent I shall take
My place among the rest, — but near the door;
Valhalla's merriment is not for me.

JOSTEJN. [Returns with a banner in his hand.]
See, now the bark is ready, as you bade.

ASGAUT. O, what a glorious end! Many a man
Will envy you, indeed.

GANDALF. [To BLANKA.] Farewell!

BLANKA. Farewell!
Farewell for life and for eternity!

RODERIK. [Struggling with himself.] Wait! Wait!

[Prostrates himself before BLANKA.]

RODERIK. Mercy, I cry! Forgive, forgive me!

BLANKA. O God!

GANDALF. What means he?

RODERIK. All will I confess:
My whole life here with you has been deceit!

BLANKA. Ah, terror has unhinged his mind!
RODERIK. No, no!

RODERIK. [To GANDALF, after he has risen.]
You are released forever from your vow;
Your father's shadow needs no blood revenge!

GANDALF. Ah, then explain!

BLANKA. Oh, speak!

RODERIK. Here stands King Rorek!

SOME. The fallen king?

BLANKA. O heavens!

GANDALF. [In doubt.] You, — my father?

RODERIK. See, Asgaut! Do you still recall the scratch
You gave me on our earliest viking trip,
The time we fought about the booty?

[He uncovers his arm and shows it to ASGAUT.]

ASGAUT. Yes,
By Thor, it is King Rorek!

GANDALF. [Throws himself in his arms.] Father! Father!
A second time now have you given me life.
My humble thanks!

RODERIK. [Downcast; to BLANKA.] And you now — what will you
Grant the old robber?

BLANKA. Love as hitherto!
I am your daughter! Has not three years' care
Wiped off each spot of blood upon your shield?

ASGAUT. Yet now explain, — how comes it that you live!

GANDALF. She saved his life.

RODERIK. Yes, like a friendly elf
She healed my wounds and cared for me,
And all the while she told me of the faith
These quiet people in the South believe,
Until my rugged heart itself was moved.
And day by day I kept the truth from her;
I did not dare to tell her —

GANDALF. But the mound there?

RODERIK. I laid therein my armor and my sword,
It seemed to me the grim old savage viking
Was buried then and there. Each day my child
Sent up a prayer for him beside the mound.

ASGAUT. Farewell!

GANDALF. Where do you go?

ASGAUT. Northward again!
I now see clearly that my time is past —
So likewise is the viking life. I go
To Iceland; there the plague has not yet come.

ASGAUT. [To BLANKA.] You, woman, take my place beside the king!
For Thor is gone — and Mjölnir out of gear;
Through you now Balder rules. — Farewell!

[He goes.]

GANDALF. Yes, Balder ruleth now, through you, my Blanka!
I see the meaning of my viking life!
'Twas not alone desire for fame and wealth
That drove me hence from my forefathers' home;
No, that which called me was a secret longing,
A quiet yearning after Balder. See,
Now is the longing stilled, now go we home;

There will I live in peace among my people.

GANDALF. [To the VIKINGS.] And will you follow?

ALL. We will follow you!

GANDALF. And you, my Blanka?

BLANKA. I? I too am born
A Northern child; for on your mountain sides
The choicest flowers of my heart took root.
To you it was I journeyed in my dreams,
From you it was that I received my love.

RODERIK. And now away!

GANDALF. But you?

BLANKA. He comes with us!

RODERIK. I shall remain.

[He points to the mound.]

RODERIK. My barrow waits for me.

BLANKA. And should I leave you here alone?

HEMMING. No, no!
Be not afraid! For I shall close his eyes
And sing to him a saga from the mound;
My last song it will be.

HEMMING. [Moved as he seizes GANDALF's hand.]
Farewell, my king!
Now have you found a better scald than I.

RODERIK. [With firmness.]
It must be so, my Gandalf; you are king,
And you have sacred duties to discharge.

[He puts their hands together.]

RODERIK. You are the children of the coming dawn, —
Go yonder where the royal throne awaits you;
I am the last one of the by-gone age,
My throne — it is the barrow — grant me that!

[GANDALF and BLANKA throw themselves silently into his arms. RODERIK ascends the burial mound. — HEMMING with his harp seats himself at his feet.]

GANDALF. [With resolution.] And now to Norway!

HROLLOUG. Home!

ALL. To Norway! Home!

BLANKA. [Fired as she seizes the banner from JOSTEJN's hand.]
Yes, now away! Our course shall northward run
O'er ocean billow on through storm and sun.
Soon fades the daylight o'er the glacier's peak,
Soon is the viking life a memory bleak!
Already sits the hero on his mound;
The time is past when he could sail around
With sword and battle cry from strand to strand.
Thor's hammer will no longer rule the land,
The North will be itself a giant grave.
But bear in mind the pledge All-Fader gave:
When moss and flowers shall the barrow hide,
To Idavold the hero's ghost shall ride, —
Then Norway too shall from the grave be brought
To chastened deeds within the realm of thought!

* * * * *

OLAF LILJEKRANS

A Play in Three Acts

1857

* * * * *

DRAMATIS PERSONÆ

LADY KIRSTEN LILJEKRANS.

OLAF LILJEKRANS Her son.

ARNE OF GULDVIK.

INGEBORG His daughter.

HEMMING His page.

THORGJERD An old fiddler.

ALFHILD.

Wedding GUESTS.

RELATIVES of Arne of Guldvik.

MAIDS and SERVANTS of Lady Kirsten.

* * * * *

SETTING

The action takes place in the middle ages, in a mountain, district.

* * * * *

FIRST ACT

[A thickly wooded hillside which leads up to higher mountain regions; in a deep ravine a swift river runs from the background out to the right; over the river lie some old logs and other remnants of a dilapidated bridge. Huge rocks lie scattered in the foreground; far away can be seen the summits of snow-capped mountain peaks. Evening twilight rests over the landscape; later on the moon appears.]

SCENE I

[THORGJERD stands on a rocky projection near the river and listens to the various choruses which are heard off the stage.]

CHORUS OF LADY KIRSTEN'S RETINUE. [Deep in the wood to the
right.]
With ringing of bells we hurry along,
We wander in field and in dell;
O Christian, come, give heed to our song,
Awake from your magic spell.

RELATIVES OF ARNE OF GULDVIK. [Far away to the right.]
Now hasten we all
To the wedding hall;
The foal runneth light and gay!
The hoofs resound
On the grassy ground
As the merry swains gallop away!

LADY KIRSTEN'S RETINUE. [A little nearer than before.]
We conjure you forth from mountain and hill,

From the places which hold you bound.
Awake to our call, come, free your will
From elves that hover around!

[THORGJERD disappears in the ravine where the river runs; after a rapid interplay the choruses are heard much nearer.]

ARNE'S RELATIVES. Our way we shorten with jest and with song,
And all of the bridal night.

LADY KIRSTEN'S RETINUE. With tears we wander the whole day long,
We search to the left and the right.

ARNE'S RELATIVES. [In close proximity, yet still outside the scene.] To wedding and banquet, to song and dance, Both servants and hand-maidens throng.

LADY KIRSTEN'S RETINUE. [Nearer than before.]
Olaf Liljekrans! Olaf Liljekrans!
Why sleep you so deep and so long?

* * * * *

SCENE II

[ARNE of Guldvik appears with his relatives, men and women, minstrels, etc., in the background to the right on the other side of the river; they are all in festive attire. Shortly afterwards HEM-MING from the same side.]

ONE OF THE RETINUE. See, here goes the way.

ANOTHER. No, here!

A THIRD. Not at all, it must be here.

ARNE OF GULDVIK. Well, well, are we now astray again!

ARNE OF GULDVIK. [Calls.] Hemming! Where is Hemming?

HEMMING. [Enters.] Here!

ARNE. Have I not told you to keep yourself close so as to be of some service to me?

HEMMING. It was Mistress Ingeborg — she wanted, — and so —

ARNE. [Annoyed.] Mistress Ingeborg! Mistress Ingeborg! Are you Mistress Ingeborg's maid? You are my page; it is me you shall serve. Do you not get your keep and wage therefor? Come, tell us where the way goes, — we are stuck.

HEMMING. [Uncertain.] The way? Well now, I am little acquainted up here, but —

ARNE. I might have known it, — that is always the service you give me! Well, we shall have to spend the night in the wilderness, as sure as I am Arne of Guldvik.

HEMMING. [Who has in the meantime spied the remnants of the bridge.] Aha, no need of that; here we can get across.

ARNE. Why didn't you tell us so in the first place?

[All cross the river and come forward on the stage.]

ARNE. [Looks about.] Yes, now I have my bearings again. The river there is the boundary between Lady Kirsten's dominions and mine.

ARNE. [Points to the left.] Down there lies her estate; in another hour or two we can sit cozily in the bridal house, but then we must hurry along.

ARNE. [Calls.] Ingeborg! — Hemming! Now where's Ingeborg?

HEMMING. In the rear, up on the hillside.

HEMMING. [Points to the right.] She is playing with her bridesmaids; they gather green twigs from the cherry trees and run about with joy and laughter.

ARNE. [Bitterly but in subdued voice.] Hemming! this wedding makes me sick; there are so many vexations about it.

ARNE. [Gazes out to the right.] There they run,—just look at them! It was she who hit upon the idea of going over the mountain instead of following the highway; we should reach our goal the sooner, she thought;—and yet notwithstanding—hm! I could go mad over it; tomorrow is she to go to the altar. Are these the decorous customs she ought to observe! What will Lady Kirsten say when she finds my daughter so ill disciplined?

ARNE. [As HEMMING starts to speak.] Yes, for that she is; she is ill disciplined, I say.

HEMMING. Master! You should never have married your daughter into Lady Kirsten's family; Lady Kirsten and her kinsmen are high-born people—

ARNE. You art stupid, Hemming! High-born, high-born! Much good that will do,—it neither feeds nor enriches a man. If Lady Kirsten is high-born, then I am rich; I have gold in my chests and silver in my coffers.

HEMMING. Yes, but your neighbors make merry over the agreement you have concluded with her.

ARNE. Ah, let them, let them; it is all because they wish me ill.

HEMMING. They say that you have surrendered your legal right in order to have Ingeborg married to Olaf Liljekrans; I shouldn't mention it, I suppose,—but a lampoon about you is going the rounds, master!

ARNE. You lie in your throat; there is no one dares make a lampoon about Arne of Guldvik. I have power; I can oust him from house and home whenever I please. Lampoon! And what do you know about lampoons!—If they have composed any songs, it is to the honor of the bride and her father!

ARNE. [Flaring up.] But it is a wretched bit of verse nevertheless, really a wretched bit of verse, I tell you. It is no man skilled in the art of poetry who has put it together, and if I once get hold of him, then—

HEMMING. Aha, master! then you know it too? Is there some one who has dared sing it to you?

ARNE. Sing, sing! Now don't stand there and delay me with your twaddle.

ARNE. [To the others.] Away, my kinsmen; little must we delay if we are to reach the bridal house before midnight. You should have heard what Hemming is telling. He says there is a rumor around that Lady Kirsten has baked and brewed for five whole days in honor of our coming. Is it not so, Hemming?

HEMMING. Aye, master!

ARNE. He says she owns not the beaker of silver so costly but she places it on the table shining and polished; so splendid a feast she has not prepared since the king came to visit her blessed lord twenty years ago. Is it not true, Hemming?

HEMMING. Aye, master!

HEMMING. [Whispering.] But, master, it is ill-thought to say such things; Lady Kirsten is proud of her birth; she thinks this marriage is somewhat of an honor to you; little you know how she intends to show herself to her guests.

ARNE. [Softly.] Ah, what nonsense!

ARNE. [To the others.] He says Lady Kirsten gives herself no rest; both day and night she is busy in pantry and cellar. Is it not —?

ARNE. [Startled as he looks out to the right.] Hemming! what is that? See here, who is that coming?

HEMMING. [With a cry.] Lady Kirsten Liljekrans!

ALL. [Astonished.] Lady Kirsten!

* * * * *

SCENE III

[The Preceding. LADY KIRSTEN comes with her HOUSE CARLS from the left.]

LADY KIRSTEN. [To her followers, without noticing the others.]
Now just a little farther and I am sure we shall find him.

LADY KIRSTEN. [Taken aback, aside.] Arne of Guldvik! Heaven
help me!

ARNE. [As he goes to meet her.] The peace of God, Lady Kirsten
Liljekrans!

LADY KIRSTEN. [Composes herself and gives him her hand.]
The peace of God to you!

LADY KIRSTEN. [Aside.] Does he then know nothing?

ARNE. [Contentedly.] And well met at the boundary! Indeed, this
pleases me; yet almost too great is the honor you show me.

LADY KIRSTEN. What mean you?

ARNE. I mean too great is the honor you show me, when you
travel miles over fields and wildernesses in order to bid me welcome on your land.

LADY KIRSTEN. Ah, Lord Arne—

LADY KIRSTEN. [Aside.] He knows nothing as yet!

ARNE. And that on a day like this, when you have enough things
to attend to; 'tis at your house we celebrate the wedding of our children, since my estate lies too far from the church, and yet you come
here to meet me with all your servants.

LADY KIRSTEN. [Embarrassed.] I beg you, say no more about
that.

ARNE. Aye, I will speak of it loudly; the village people have said
that you pride yourself on your noble birth, that you look down
upon me and mine, and that you entered into the agreement only in
order to put an end to the long-standing disputes which grew trou-
blesome now that you have become a widow and begin to grow old;
and if that had not been the case, you would never—

LADY KIRSTEN. How can you listen to what evil tongues in-
vent? No more will we think of our differences which have lasted

since the days of your ancestors. I think our families have suffered enough these years, yours as well as mine. Look around you, Lord Arne! Is not the hillside here like the wildest of upland pastures? And yet in our fathers' days it was a region much frequented and rich. A bridge there was across the river, and a highway from Guldvik to my father's house. But with fire and sword they sallied forth from both sides; they laid everything waste that they came upon, for it seemed to them that they were too near neighbors. Now all sorts of weeds grow in the highway, the bridge is broken, and it is only the bear and the wolf that make their homes here.

ARNE. Yes, they ran the road around the mountain below; it is a good deal longer and they could thus better keep an eye on one another; but there is little need of that now, — which is well and good for both of us.

LADY KIRSTEN. To be sure, to be sure! But Ingeborg, the bride, where is she? I do not see her, and the bridesmaids likewise are lacking; surely she is not—

ARNE. She follows in the rear; she must shortly be here. But— listen, Lady Kirsten! One thing I will tell you, as well first as last, although, I should think, you know it. Ingeborg has at times whims and moods, — I swear to you she has them, however well disciplined she may be.

LADY KIRSTEN. [Expectant.] Well, what then?

LADY KIRSTEN. [Aside.] Is she too—

ARNE. Such things you must tame; I, as her father, will never succeed, but you will no doubt find ways and means.

LADY KIRSTEN. Aye, rest you assured.

LADY KIRSTEN. [Aside.] And Olaf, who is nowhere to be seen!

HEMMING. [Who has looked out to the right.] There comes Mistress Ingeborg.

HEMMING. [Aside.] How fair she is advancing foremost in the group!

LADY KIRSTEN. [Slowly to her servants.] You will keep silent about your errand up here.

A SERVANT. You may be sure of that.

HEMMING. [Aside, sighing, as he continues to look out to the right.] Ah, happy is Olaf, who will have her!

* * * * *

SCENE IV

[The Preceding. INGEBORG and the Bridesmaids come over the bridge.]

INGEBORG. [Still in the background.] Why do you run away from me? What good will that do? There can be no wedding anyway before I come.

INGEBORG. [Notices LADY KIRSTEN and her retinue.] Lady Kirsten! you here? Well, I am glad of that.

[Casually to the retinue.]

[To LADY KIRSTEN as she looks about.]

LADY KIRSTEN. Olaf!

LADY KIRSTEN. [Aside.] Woe is me! now it will out.

ARNE. Yes, Olaf, indeed! Ha, ha, ha! I must have been blind; 'tis well the bride sees better than I; for I have not noticed that the bridegroom is lacking; but now I understand very well how it comes that we meet here, — it is he who is causing —

LADY KIRSTEN. He — you mean — you know, that —

ARNE. I mean it has grown tedious for him down there in the festive hall. Aye, aye, I remember now my own wedding day; at that time I also was young. He has had a great desire to meet the bride, and accordingly he prevailed upon you to go with him.

LADY KIRSTEN. He greatly desired, to be sure, to meet the bride, but —

152

INGEBORG. But what?

LADY KIRSTEN. Olaf is not here with us.

HEMMING. [Approaches.] Not with you!

ARNE. And why not?

INGEBORG. Speak, I beg you!

LADY KIRSTEN. [Embarrassed and jestingly.] Truly, it appears the bride also is anxious! Come along, come along with me down to the bridal hall; there, I imagine he will be found.

HEMMING. [Whispering to ARNE.] Master! remember I gave you warning.

ARNE. [Suspiciously to LADY KIRSTEN.] First answer me; then shall we follow.

LADY KIRSTEN. Well then, — he is ridden out to the hunt.

LADY KIRSTEN. [As she is about to go.] Come, 'tis fast growing dark.

INGEBORG. To the hunt?

LADY KIRSTEN. Aye! Does that surprise you? You know the song of course:
  "The knight likes to ride in the forest around,
  To test his horse and his hound!"

INGEBORG. Does he think so little of his young bride that he uses the wedding days to go hunting wild animals?

LADY KIRSTEN. Now you are jesting. Come along, come along!

ARNE. [Who has in the meantime kept his eye on LADY KIRSTEN and her retinue.] No, wait, Lady Kirsten! I hardly dare measure myself in wisdom with you, but one thing clearly I see, and that is that you are concealing your real errand up here.

LADY KIRSTEN. [Confused.] I? How can you think that?

ARNE. From one thing and another I can see you are concealing something. You are strangely downcast, and yet you pretend to be playful in spirit; but it won't do —

LADY KIRSTEN. 'Tis nothing new for you to think ill of me and mine.

ARNE. Perhaps; but never did I do so without just cause.

ARNE. [Bursting out.] As sure as I live, there is something you are hiding from me.

LADY KIRSTEN. [Aside.] What will be the end of this?

ARNE. I let myself be fooled by you, but now I see clearly enough. You said you came to greet me at the boundary. How did you know we took the way over the mountain? It was Ingeborg who suggested this way just as we left Guldvik, and no one could have informed you about it.

ARNE. [When LADY KIRSTEN does not answer.] You are silent, as I might have known.

HEMMING. [In an undertone.] You see, master! Will you now believe what I said?

ARNE. [Likewise.] Hush!

LADY KIRSTEN. [Who has in the meantime composed herself.] Well and good, Lord Arne! I will be honest with you; let chance take care of the rest.

ARNE. Then tell us —

INGEBORG. What mean you?

LADY KIRSTEN. The agreement between us is sealed with word and with hand, — many honorable men whom I see here can bear witness to that: Olaf, my son, was to wed your daughter; tomorrow at my house the wedding was to be held —

ARNE. [Impatiently.] Yes, yes!

LADY KIRSTEN. Dishonor to him who breaks his word, but —

ARNE AND THE GUESTS.. What then! Speak out!

LADY KIRSTEN. There can be no wedding tomorrow as we had agreed.

ARNE. No wedding?

LADY KIRSTEN. It must be postponed.

HEMMING. Ah, shame and disgrace!

INGEBORG. No wedding!

ARNE. Cursed be you that you play me false!

THE GUESTS. [Threatening, as several of them draw their knives and rush in on Lady Kirsten's people.] Revenge! Revenge on the house of Liljekrans!

LADY KIRSTEN'S MEN. [Raise their axes and prepare to defend themselves.] Strike too! Down with the men of Guldvik!

LADY KIRSTEN. [Throws herself between the contending parties.] Stop, stop; I pray you, stop! Lord Arne! hear me to the end ere you judge my conduct.

ARNE. [Who has tried to quiet his kinsmen, approaches LADY KIRSTEN and speaks in a low tone as he tries to overcome his inner agitation, which is nevertheless apparent.] Forgive me, Lady Kirsten! I was too quick in my wrath. Had I stopped to think I might surely have known the whole was a jest on your part; I beg you, do not contradict me, it must be so! No wedding tomorrow,—how could such a thing happen! If it is ale and mead you lack, or if you need silver or embroidered linens, then come you to me.

LADY KIRSTEN. It is no poor man's house that your daughter is marrying into, Lord Arne! Do you but come to the wedding with all your kinsmen and friends, aye, come with three times as many if you wish,—in my home you shall find plenty of room and banquet fare, as much as you may desire. Think not for a moment that such an inglorious reason could stand in my way.

ARNE. You have changed your mind, perchance?

LADY KIRSTEN. Nor that either! If I have given my word, then am I likewise ready to keep it, today just as well as tomorrow; for such was ever the custom and rule in my family. But in this instance it is not in my power; one there is lacking—

INGEBORG. One! Whom? Surely I should think that when the bride is ready,—

LADY KIRSTEN. For a wedding two people are needed, the groom as well as the bride—

ARNE AND THE GUESTS. Olaf!

INGEBORG. My betrothed!

LADY KIRSTEN. Yes, he, my son — this night he is fled from his home and his bride.

GUESTS. Fled!

ARNE. Fled! He!

LADY KIRSTEN. As I hope for the grace of heaven, I have no hand therein.

ARNE. [With suppressed exasperation.] And the wedding was to be tomorrow! My daughter has put on her golden attire; invitations I have sent around in the district; my kinsmen and friends come from far away to attend the festive day.

ARNE. [Flaring up.] Ah, take you good care, if Arne of Guldvik is held up to scorn before his neighbors; it shall profit you little, — that I solemnly swear!

LADY KIRSTEN. You reason unjustly, if you think —

ARNE. 'Tis not, Lady Kirsten, for you to say so! We two have an old account to settle; it is not the first time that you set your cunning traps for me and mine. The race of Guldvik has long had to suffer, when you and your kinsmen plotted deception and guile. Power we had, — we had wealth and property too; but you were too crafty for us. You knew how to lure us with wily words and ready speech, — those are wares I am little able to reckon as I should.

LADY KIRSTEN. Lord Arne! Hear me, I pray!

ARNE. [Continuing.] Now I see clearly that I have behaved like the man who built his house on the ice-floe: a thaw came on and down he went to the bottom. But you shall have little joy of this. I shall hold you to account, Lady Kirsten! You must answer for your son; you it was who made love for him, and your affair it will be to keep the word you have given me! A fool I was, aye, tenfold a fool, that I put my faith in your glib tongue. Those who wished me well gave me warning; my enemies made me an object of scorn; but little heed gave I to either. I put on my gala attire; kinsmen and friends I

156

gathered together; with song and laughter we set out for the festive hall, and then, — the bridegroom has fled.

INGEBORG. Never will I marry one who holds me so lightly.

ARNE. Be still!

HEMMING. [Softly to ARNE.] Mistress Ingeborg is right; best it is you break the agreement.

ARNE. Be still, I say!

LADY KIRSTEN. [To ARNE.] You may well be rilled with wrath and resentment; but if you think I meant to deceive you, you do me the greatest injustice. You think we are playing a game of deception with you. But tell me, — what would tempt me and my son to such a thing? Does he not love Ingeborg? Where could he choose him a better bride? Is she not fair and lithe? Is her father not rich and mighty? Is not her family mentioned with honor as far as it is known?

ARNE. But how then could Olaf—

LADY KIRSTEN. The lot I have suffered is worse than you think. You will pity me instead of growing angry when you have heard. — Since the sun rose this morning I have wandered up here to find him again.

ARNE. Up here?

LADY KIRSTEN. Yes, up here; I must tell you — you'll be frightened — but nevertheless, — Olaf is bewitched in the mountain!

GUESTS. Bewitched in the mountain!

INGEBORG. [At the same time.] Deliver me, God!

ARNE. What say you, Lady Kirsten?

LADY KIRSTEN. He is bewitched in the mountain! Nothing else can it be. — Three weeks ago, after the betrothal feast at Guldvik, he did not come home till far into the next day. Pale he was and moody and quiet as I had never seen him before. And thus the days went by; he spoke but little; he lay in his bed most of the time and turned his face to the wall; but when evening came on, it seemed a strange uneasiness seized him; he saddled his horse and rode away, far up the mountain side; but no one dared follow him, and no one knew where he went beyond that. Believe me, 'tis evil spirits that have charmed his mind; great is the power they wield in here; from the time the terrible plague overran the country it has never been quite safe in the mountain here; there is scarcely a day goes by but the chalet girls hear strange playing and music, although there is no living soul in the place whence it comes.

ARNE. Bewitched in the mountain! Could such a thing be possible?

LADY KIRSTEN. Would to God it were not; but I can no longer doubt it. Three days is it now since he last was at home.

ARNE. And you have seen none who knows where he is?

LADY KIRSTEN. Alas, no, it is not so easy. Up here a hunter yesterday saw him; but he was wild and shy as the deer; he had picked all sorts of flowers, and these he scattered before him wherever he went, and all the while he whispered strange words. As soon as I heard of this, I set out with my people, but we have found nothing.

INGEBORG. You met none who could tell you —

LADY KIRSTEN. You know of course the mountain-side is desolate.

ARNE. [As he spies THORGJERD, who rises from the river.] Here comes one will I ask.

HEMMING. [Apprehensively.] Master! Master!

ARNE. What now?

HEMMING. Let him go! Do you not see who it is?

THE GUESTS AND LADY KIRSTEN'S PEOPLE. [Whispering among themselves.] Thorgjerd the fiddler! The crazy Thorgjerd!

INGEBORG. He has learned the nixie's songs.

HEMMING. Let him go, let him go!

ARNE. No, — not even were he the nixie himself —

* * * * *

SCENE V

[The Preceding.]

[THORGJERD has in the meantime gone to the edge of the stage to the left; at ARNE's last words he turns about suddenly as if he had been addressed.]

THORGJERD. [As he draws a step or two nearer.] What do you want of me?

ARNE. [Startled.] What's that?

HEMMING. Now see!

ARNE. Let me manage this.

ARNE. [To THORGJERD.] We seek Olaf Liljekrans. Have you met him about here today?

THORGJERD. Olaf Liljekrans?

LADY KIRSTEN. Why, yes, — you know him well.

THORGJERD. Is he not one of the evil men from the villages?

LADY KIRSTEN. Evil?

THORGJERD. They are all evil there! Olaf Liljekrans curses the little bird when it sings on his mother's roof.

LADY KIRSTEN. You lie, you fiddler!

THORGJERD. [With an artful smile.] So much the better for him.

ARNE. How so?

THORGJERD. You ask about Olaf Liljekrans? Has he gone astray in here? You seek him and cannot find him?

LADY KIRSTEN. Yes, yes!

THORGJERD. So much the better for him; — if it were a lie that I told, he will suffer no want.

INGEBORG. Speak out what you know!

THORGJERD. Then I should never be done!

THORGJERD. [Mischievously.] Elves and sprites hold sway here. Be you of good cheer! If you find him not he is at play with the

elves; they are fond of all who love little birds, and Olaf, you said....
Go home, — go home again. Olaf is up in the mountain; he suffers no
want.

LADY KIRSTEN. Curse you for saying such things!

ARNE. [To LADY KIRSTEN.] Do not heed what he says.

THORGJERD. [Approaches again.] I go hence now to tune my
harp; Olaf Liljekrans is up in the mountain, — there shall his wedding be held. — Mad Thorgjerd must also be there; he can make
tables and benches dance, so stirring is the music he plays. But you,
take you heed; go you home again; it is not safe for you here. Have
you not heard the old saying: Beware of the elves when they frolic
around, They may draw you into their play; And all that you see
and all that you hear Will stay with your mind alway.

THORGJERD. [Suddenly breaking out with wild joy.] But here
there are wedding guests, — ah! Each lady has on her very best
gown, each man his very best coat, — now I see. Olaf Liljekrans is
likewise a groom in the village, — there also he has a betrothed!
Well, you have heard of such things before! I know that at any rate
once, — it is years ago — but well I remember....

THORGJERD. [He continues after a moment's pause, more and
more
wildly.]
  Sir Alvar and Ingrid had plighted their troth,
  She was a sprightly maiden;
  Three blessed long days they feasted and sang,
  With jolly good wine they were laden.
  The bride was fair and the bride was gay,
  The dance of the guests she led,
  When in came the nixie, the evil wight,
  And sat on the edge of the bed.
  Like a fiddler he sat on the edge of the bed,
  And music bewitchingly played.
  Around danced the benches and tables and all,
  As lightly as servant and maid! —
  The nixie he went through the open door, —
  The truth it boots not to hide! —
  And while he played on the harpstrings sweet,

There followed him ever — the bride!

THORGJERD. [Wildly, triumphantly.]
  Fast in a spell lay knight and page,
  The groom knew not whither to go,
  The nixie made ready the bridal bed,
  Little Ingrid's bed in the river below.

THORGJERD. [Suddenly becomes quiet and says softly.] That song
I shall never forget! — But go you home, night is coming on, and
when the sun is down the forest belongs to the others. Farewell!
I shall take greetings to Olaf where he sits — in the mountain!

  [Goes out to the left.]

  * * * * *

SCENE VI

[The Preceding except THORGJERD.]

ARNE. [To LADY KIRSTEN.] He lies! Do not believe him!

HEMMING. But it is nevertheless true, — the tale of the bride who
disappeared on the eve of her wedding.

ARNE. Aye, that was many years ago; nowadays such things
never happen. But we'll all help to find him.

INGEBORG. It was not sung at my cradle that I should run about
in forest and field to find my bridegroom.

ARNE. Be still!

INGEBORG. If he is enthralled in the mountain, then let her take
him who has done it; I don't propose to share my betrothed's heart
and soul.

HEMMING. [Softly and feelingly.] The Lord bless you for those
words!

INGEBORG. [With a haughty look of dismissal.] What?

ARNE. Will you be silent, I say!

ARNE. [To the Guests.] Now quick, my good men! Spread out and search for him on every ridge and in every hillock! Away! Quite so! Tomorrow we drink to the wedding!

[The Guests and LADY KIRSTEN's People go out in different groups to the right and the left.]

ARNE. [Softly, to LADY KIRSTEN.] We must find him! It would cause me eternal shame if the wedding —

LADY KIRSTEN. Come, then, come!

INGEBORG. [Softly, to HEMMING, who stands downcast.] Why do you not go with the rest? Better it were that you brought me again my betrothed than stand here thus and bless me for words I really don't mean.

ARNE. [At the exit.] Come, come!

INGEBORG. [To HEMMING, who starts to go.] Wait, Hemming! Fasten my shoe buckle!

[LADY KIRSTEN and ARNE go out to the left.]

* * * * *

SCENE VII

[INGEBORG. HEMMING.]

INGEBORG. [Puts her foot forward.] See there, — fasten it tight!

[HEMMING kneels and does her bidding.]

INGEBORG. [As she puts the other foot forward.] There, — buckle this one too! Well, why do you bow your head? Has something gone wrong?

HEMMING. Do you demand that I shall speak honestly?

INGEBORG. Certainly I do.

HEMMING. Well, then you must know —

INGEBORG. [Quickly.] O no, it isn't necessary.

[She moves away a few steps; HEMMING rises.]

HEMMING. Alas, Lady Ingeborg! Once you were so kind to me; but now since you have become a real grown-up lady — and especially, I imagine, since you gave your betrothal vow —

INGEBORG. What then?

HEMMING. O nothing! —

[A pause.]

HEMMING. Can you remember, — we have been up here once before?

INGEBORG. [Curtly.] I don't remember!

HEMMING. You had run after your spotted goat, and I followed you, as was always my custom, — yes, that was a long time ago, but I remember it as if it happened today; right down there lies the swamp, which —

INGEBORG. [Comes nearer.] Was it the time we heard the bear?

HEMMING. Yes, the very time.

INGEBORG. [Constantly becoming more animated.] I found the goat again.

HEMMING. No, it was I who first discovered it.

INGEBORG. Yes, yes, you are right; up there on the slope —

HEMMING. And then you took your garter.

INGEBORG. And bound it.

HEMMING. Yes, for we had come to pick strawberries.

INGEBORG. Over there on the hill, yes! And you had made me a birch-bark scrip.

HEMMING. But then it was we heard —

INGEBORG. The bear, ha, ha, ha! We had to cross the swamp just where it was the wettest, —

HEMMING. And then I took you in my arms.

INGEBORG. And jumped with me from tuft to tuft.

INGEBORG. [Laughing.] How frightened we were, the two of us!

HEMMING. Of course I was most frightened for your sake.

INGEBORG. And I for yours —

[Stops suddenly and as she continues to look at him her face assumes an imperious and wounded expression.]

INGEBORG. What is it you stand here and say? Why don't you go? Is it fitting to speak thus to your master's daughter? Go, go; you were to find my betrothed!

HEMMING. Alas, I forgot your betrothed; I forgot that you are my master's daughter.

INGEBORG. If you find him, I promise you an embroidered jacket for Christmas, — so pleased shall I be.

HEMMING. I don't want any jacket; I serve you neither for gold nor silver, neither for keep nor for knightly dress. But now I am off; what lies in my power I shall do, if I know it pleases you.

INGEBORG. [Who has climbed up on a stone and is picking some blossoming cherry twigs.] Hemming! how rich is my betrothed?

HEMMING. How rich he is I really can't say; but it is said of his grandsire in the song: With golden attire he can provide A hundred maids or more for his bride! So mighty perhaps is not Olaf Liljekrans, but still he owns both forest and field.

INGEBORG. [Still occupied.] And you, what do you possess?

HEMMING. [Sighing.] My poverty — is all I have.

INGEBORG. That isn't very much, Hemming!

HEMMING. No, it isn't very much, Mistress Ingeborg!

INGEBORG. [Hums, turned away from him, without changing her position, and still occupied as before.]
'Tis little my heart is attracted indeed

To him who has all the wealth he may need!
Much more I fancy the humble swain,
The friend of my heart he will ever remain!

HEMMING. [In the greatest joy.] Ingeborg! O, if what you say is true, I must tenfold bless my poverty.

INGEBORG. [Turns her head and speaks coldly.] I don't understand you; the song was only an ancient ballad.

[Comes down from the rock with the cherry twigs in her hand, and approaches him as she looks at him fixedly.]

INGEBORG. But I know another song too, and that I will sing for you:
The king's court within stand the steeds so fair;
The suitor who lacks not the courage to dare, —
He shoes the yellow, he shoes the gray,
The swiftest he saddles before it is day!
He places his bride on the steed behind,
She follows him safe, she follows him blind.
He rides with her off, to the sea they hie,
With him she would willingly live and die!

HEMMING. [As though beside himself.] Ingeborg! Ingeborg! then nothing shall henceforth terrify me! Not that you have a betrothed, not that you are my master's daughter; — yea, as sure as I live, I shall steal you tonight!

INGEBORG. [Vehemently, as she constantly struggles to suppress a smile.] Help me, God! what is amiss with you? What is it you are thinking of? Will you steal your master's daughter? You must be sick or mad to conceive such a thing! Yet, it shall be forgotten — for this once. Go, now! and thank heaven you escape so lightly; for you have certainly earned a blow —

INGEBORG. [Raises the twigs, but lets them fall, and says in a changed tone.] — and my red golden ring — see there, take it!

[Throws him a ring, which she has removed from her arm, and rushes out quickly to the left.]

* * * * *

SCENE VIII

[HEMMING. Shortly afterwards OLAF Liljekrans from the, background. The moon rises.]

HEMMING. The golden ring unto me she has granted,
Then still is she true, I am not deceived!
'Twas only in jest that she scolded and ranted
As though she were bitterly grieved.
All will I venture, no more will I dread!

HEMMING. [Despondent.] And yet, I am only a penniless swain,
And early tomorrow is she to be wed!

HEMMING. [Quickly.] But into the forest the bridegroom is fled;
O, if he should never come home again!

HEMMING. [Starts to rush out, but stops with a cry.]
Olaf! there is he!

[OLAF comes slowly forward between the rocks in the background. He walks dreaming, his head uncovered, and his hands full of flowers which he tears to pieces and scatters on the way; his whole behavior during the following indicates an unsettled mind.]

OLAF. [Without noticing HEMMING.]
If only I knew What she meant, could somehow the riddle unravel!

[Starts to go out to the left.]

HEMMING. Lord Olaf! Lord Olaf! O where do you travel?
O hear me, Lord Olaf!

OLAF. [Half awakening.]
Hemming! Is it you? Stand not in my way!

HEMMING. What is it that weighs
On your mind, that you wander in here for three days?

   [Observes him more closely.]

HEMMING. And what is the game that here you do play, —
Your cheek is white, and your forehead is gray!

OLAF. Be not so amazed that my cheek is white,
Three nights have I fought so strange a fight;
Be not so amazed that my forehead is gray,
Three nights have I been in the elfen play.

   HEMMING. Heaven protect us!

OLAF. I am ill, I am faint!
I remember neither devil nor saint!

HEMMING. [Apprehensively.]
Come, Olaf, with me to your mother's estate!

OLAF. My mother's estate! Where stood it of late?
'Tis here, as it seems, that I have my home!
The wood has become my ancestral hall,
The river's roaring, the pine-trees' moan,
Is sweeter to me than my mother's call.

OLAF. [With increasing rapture.]
Aye, here it is quiet! Aye, here it is fair!
Behold, my hall for the feast I prepare.

   HEMMING. [Aside.] O what has come o'er him?

   OLAF. Soon comes my bride!

HEMMING. Your bride! Then you know — ?

OLAF. [Continuing.] When the day has died,
When slumber the birds, when fades the cloud,
Then here will she come so young and so proud!

HEMMING. [Crosses himself.]
All heavenly saints! I fear the worst!

OLAF. Know you when it was that I saw her here first?
I rode late one evening from Guldvik hall,
Some kind of feast I seem to recall.
My spirit was heavy, my heart full of woe!
That something had grieved me is all that I know.
I rode all alone up the mountain side,
At midnight I passed by the river so wide;
Then heard I beyond a melodious wail,
That rang like a song over mountain and dale.
It seemed a plaintive, bewitching lay;
I folded my hands, I tried to pray,
But tied was my tongue and my thoughts went astray;
The strains did beguile and lure me away.
'Twas now like weeping and now like laughter,
'Twas now full of mirth, and now ever after
As were it the cry of a perishing man,
As were it a soul in the anguish of death,
That I heard in the song so beguiling, that ran
Like a stream around me! — I scarce got my breath!
So sorely bewildered was I in my soul;
It was as if powers both gentle and strong
Enticed me and lured me away from my goal,
I needs must come up, I was carried along.
And ever rang out the mysterious call;
How far I rode on I no longer recall.

HEMMING. [Aside.] And the bride, of whom the minstrel
sang, — she too had to follow —

OLAF. My foal stopped short, I awoke in a maze,
I looked around with a wondering gaze;
'Twas all so pleasant and fair! But what land
I was in I could not understand!
I stood in a valley;—a deep peace lay
Over all like dew in the night!
The moon on the edge of the tarn did play;
It seemed to laugh as it vanished away
In the rolling billows so bright!
My head was heavy, my spirit oppressed,
I yearned for nothing but sleep;
I laid me down 'neath a linden to rest
In the whispering forest so sweet!

    HEMMING. Lord Olaf! Lord Olaf! How dared you do it?

OLAF. [Continuing.]
I ventured then into the elf-maidens' play;
The fairest of maidens gave me a bouquet
Of snow-drops blue and of lilies white;
She pierced my soul with her glances so bright,
And whispered to me what nobody knows,—
A word I'll keep ever in mind:
"Olaf Liljekrans! know you where happiness grows,
Know you the hour when peace you will find?
Of all the flowers on the hill over yonder
Must you the fairest one find,
And bit by bit you must tear it asunder
And scatter it far to the wind,
Then—only then will you happiness find!"

    HEMMING. You have slumbered and dreamed!

OLAF. That very same day
My mother's estate grew cramped and narrow!
Through thicket, o'er highway, I hastened away
To the grove so pleasant with bow and with arrow!
There met I again the elf-maiden fair.

HEMMING. [Steps back amazed.] When then, — have you wakened and found — ?

OLAF. I took my betrothal ring, shot with it there
Right over her head, far into the air;
Now is she evermore bound!

HEMMING. And it is the bride you are waiting for here?

OLAF. Yes, yes, the bride; soon will she be near!

HEMMING. [Aside.] His soul is enthralled, his mind is ill;
All this Lady Kirsten shall know!

HEMMING. [Aloud.] And dare you go wandering fearless up here
In the hills?

OLAF. It is here so still,
'Tis sweetly I dream as I go!

[Goes slowly in between the huge rocks in front on the right.]

HEMMING. His wedding tomorrow his people prepare;
Yet for his betrothed he seems little to care;
'Tis little he knows that she is so near,
And less that she holds another one dear! —
He wanders around in the forest astray,
And Ingeborg gave me the golden ring!
His mother I'll seek without further delay;
The saints only know what the morrow will bring!

[Goes out to the left.]

* * * * *

SCENE IX

[OLAF LILJEKRANS enters again from the right.]

OLAF. [As he tears to pieces some flowers he has gathered off the stage.] "Of all the flowers on the hill over yonder
Must you the fairest one find;
And bit by bit you must tear it asunder,
And scatter it far to the wind, —
Then — only then will you happiness find!"
These mysterious words give my spirit no rest.
The fairest of flowers? And what is the test?
Where will it be found? Is its beauty revealed
In the fragrance or deep in the blossom concealed?
Or hid in some magic power that I never
Can possibly find if I search forever?
So may there be virtue in many a spear
Whose steel is rusty and out of gear;
So too may a harp that no longer sings
But hangs forgotten in the halls of mirth,
Hide in its forsaken and dusty strings
The strangest magic on earth.

* * * * *

SCENE X

[OLAF LILJEKRANS. ALFHILD from the back of the stage. She is fantastically dressed and adorned with flowers and garlands of leaves; she looks about anxiously until she discovers OLAF and runs joyfully to meet him.]

ALFHILD. O, stay, stay! Do not go away from me!

OLAF. [As if suddenly awakened to life.] Alfhild! my young and beautiful bride!

ALFHILD. Olaf! my handsome knight! I grew tired of waiting; I had to come here to meet you!

OLAF. But tell me, why are you always afraid to come here?

ALFHILD. I have so often told you that I never went beyond this valley until you visited me. My father has said that evil powers hold sway out there; only here among the mountains could I fare safely and without harm! O, let whatever power will hold sway; you are here, and that is enough for me! Come, let me look into your eyes! Truly, I have you again!

OLAF. Have me! Alas, Alfhild! You artful, you beautiful woman, indeed you have me again! My soul you have charmed so deeply, so deeply. Lead me whither and as far as you will, into the mountain, under the hill, to the grassy meadow, where song and refrain echo sweetly in the evening, on the bottom of the river, down under the rapids, where there are harps for powerful plaintive lays; wherever your home is, there I am ready to wander!

ALFHILD. Why speak you thus? You must surely know better than what you are saying.—Spirits and elves hold sway in mountain and hillock, and on the bottom of the river lives the nixie,—so father has said. Think you that I am an elf or—

OLAF. You are the fairest in the world; be you what you please, so long as you are mine!

ALFHILD. Were I an elfen maid, then truly, say I, it would fare with you ill!

OLAF. Me!

ALFHILD. Yes, you! When you rode on your lonely path, I should go out to meet you and give you the drink of forgetfulness from the golden horn. I should mix therein my magic and charm so that you would forget both heaven and earth, forget where you were born and reared, what name you answered to, and where your kinsmen fared,—one thing alone should you remember, one thing alone should fill your mind and soul.

OLAF. Forsooth, then are you the elfen maid! For from the first hour you have practiced your magic on me.

ALFHILD. Have I?

OLAF. Through the meadow I rode, below where the river runs,—it was night and the songs and the plaintive lays echoed strangely around me....

OLAF. Bewildered I grew and lost my path; I wandered far, far in among the mountains; I discovered the beautiful valley, where no foot has trod, where no eye has feasted ere mine....

OLAF. A heavy slumber fell upon me in there; the elf maidens played in the meantime, and they drew me into their play....

OLAF. But when I awoke, there was affliction in my soul; homeward I rode, but down there I could no more be content; it seemed as if I had left behind me the richest and best in life, as if a wonderful treasure were held in store for me, if only I sought and found it....

OLAF. Up to the valley I had to go before I could find peace....

OLAF. You came to meet me, fair and glowing as in this hour; I seized your hand, I looked you in the eye — heaven and earth, the beauty of all creation, was in your eye!....

OLAF. Then I forgot both kinsmen and friends!....

OLAF. I came there the next night, I embraced you, I pressed you to my bosom, — the glory of heaven was in your embrace....

OLAF. — Then I forgot my Christian name and my forefathers' home....

OLAF. And I came the third night; I had to come; I kissed your red lips; my eyes burned their way into your soul. — More than the glory of creation was therein! I forgot more than God and home, more than heaven and earth. I forgot myself.

[Prostrates himself before her.]

OLAF. Alfhild! Alfhild!

ALFHILD. If it be a drink of forgetfulness which you speak of, then have I also charmed myself with it. I have fared as the minstrel who learned the nixie's songs in order to charm his sweetheart; — he charmed and charmed so long that at length the magic wove itself round his own soul too, and he could never win himself free therefrom.

[Stops and continues standing thoughtfully.]

OLAF. [As he rises.] What are you brooding over?

ALFHILD. High in the mountain there is a rocky ledge so steep that not even the eagle can fasten his claws thereon; there stands a lonely birch, — ill does it thrive, it is poor in leaves; but downward it bends its branches to the valley which lies far away; it is as though it longed for its sisters in the fresh and luxuriant grove, as though it yearned to be transplanted in the warm sunny life down below....

ALFHILD. Like the birch in the mountain was also my life; I longed to get away; I longed for you through the long, long years, even before I knew you existed. The valley became too cramped for me, but I did not know that beyond the mountains there was another valley like this one in here. The knights and the ladies that visited me every evening were not enough for me, and they told me nothing of the life beyond!

OLAF. Knights and ladies? You told me you never met any one there.

ALFHILD. No one like you! But every evening my father sang songs to me, and when the night came and my eyes were closed, they came to visit me, all those that live in my father's songs. Merry knights and beautiful ladies there were among them; they came with falcons on their hands, riding on stately steeds. They danced in the field, and laughter and merriment reechoed wherever they fared; the elves listened silently from behind each flower and the birds from the trees where they had fallen asleep. But with the coming of dawn they again disappeared; lonely I wandered; I decked myself with flowers and with green leaves, for I knew the next night they would come again. Alas, that life was after all not sufficient for me; a mighty longing rilled my bosom; it would never have been stilled if you had not come!

OLAF. You speak of your father; at no time did I see him in there!

ALFHILD. But seldom he comes now; he has never been there since the night we first met.

OLAF. But tell me, where is he?

ALFHILD. You have told me you rode late one summer night in the meadow where the river flows; there you heard strange songs which you only half understood, but which haunt and haunt you so that you will never forget them.

OLAF. Yes, yes!

ALFHILD. You once heard my father's songs! It is on them that I have been nourished. In truth, neither have I fully understood them; they seemed to me to be the most precious treasure, to be life itself; now they mean little to me; they are to me but a token of all the glory that was to come. In all of them was there a handsome knight; I imagined him to be the best and most glorious thing in all the valleys, the best and most glorious as far as bird can fly, as far as clouds can sail. Olaf! it was you, — I know you again! Oh, you must tell me of your home, of the distant valley whence you come; life out there must be rich and glorious; there it must be that my birds all fly with the falling of the leaves; for when they again come to visit me, they have so much to tell that is strange, so many a marvel to sing about, that all the flowers begin to bud and to blossom, the trees to grow green, and the big and glorious sun to rise early and go tardily to rest, in order to listen to all the stories and songs. But little grasp I of all that they tell; you must interpret it for me, you must make everything clear that inwardly craves an answer.

OLAF. Little am I able to answer what you ask of my home. My home? If I have had a home other than this, then I remember but little about it. It is all to me like a misty dream which is forgotten in the hour we waken. Yet, come! far below us there lies a village; there it seems I remember I wandered before I saw you; there it seems to me that my kinsmen live. Do you hear how the river conjures and rushes; let us follow it; out on the ledge near the waterfall we can overlook the village where I — once had my home. Come, come!

ALFHILD. But dare I —

OLAF. Follow and trust me, I shall protect you!

ALFHILD. I am ready; I know it well enough; whether I wished to or not, I must follow you wherever you go.

[They go out to the right.]

CHORUS OF WEDDING GUESTS AND LADY. KIRSTEN'S PEOPLE

      (From the forest to the left.)
 Awake to our call, come free your will

From elves that hover around!

* * * * *

SCENE XI

[LADY KIRSTEN and HEMMING enter from the left.]

HEMMING. Here he was; — why — now he is gone!

LADY KIRSTEN. And he said he was waiting for the bride who was to come?

HEMMING. Yes, but whom he had in mind I could not quite make out; for his speech was strangely incoherent. Ingeborg he did not mean, — that is certain.

LADY KIRSTEN. Say nothing, good Hemming! say nothing of what he just said! You did well to let me alone know he was here. You shall be richly rewarded for this, but first we must find him again —

HEMMING. [As he looks out to the right.] See, — see there, in the moonlight, on the hill near the river, — yes, surely I think —

LADY KIRSTEN. Hush, hush, it is Olaf!

HEMMING. There are two; a woman is with him —

LADY KIRSTEN. Heavenly saints!

HEMMING. He is pointing out the village as if — there they go!

LADY KIRSTEN. Call Lord Arne and our people! We will meet again here; I bring Olaf with me!

HEMMING. But dare you then — ?

LADY KIRSTEN. Do as I say; but say nothing of what you have heard and seen. You can say that Olaf came up here to hunt deer and bear, and that he went astray in the mountain.

HEMMING. You can rely on me, Lady Kirsten!

[Goes out to the left.]

LADY KIRSTEN. Is it true, then? Have evil sprites gained control over him? Yes, so I can pretend to Arne of Guldvik, but little I believe it myself; — and yet it is said it happened often enough in the days gone by. But it is elfen maids no doubt of flesh and blood that — . There he goes down to the river, — I must hasten!

[Goes out to the right in the background.]

CHORUS. [From the forest to the left.]
  With ringing of bells we hurry along,
  We wander in field and in dell!
  O Christian, come, give heed to our song,
  Wake up from your magic spell!

   * * * * *

SCENE XII

[OLAF and ALFHILD come in from the right in the background. Later LADY KIRSTEN.]

ALFHILD. O, you must tell me still more of the world!
Your words to my soul are refreshing indeed;
It seems as if here in the wonders you tell
My innermost longings you read!....

Did you ne'er on a summer night sit by a tarn,
So deep that no one could fathom it quite,
And see in the water the stars so bright,
Those knowing eyes that express with their flickering light
Much more than a thousand tongues could possibly say?

   * * * * *

I often sat thus; I sought with my hands to capture
The sparkling riddles below in the deep —
I snatched after them, I would see them close,
Then they grew blurred like eyes that weep, —

It is idle to search and to seek—

* * * * *

So too in my soul there was many a riddle
I yearned to solve in the days that are gone!
They tricked me as did all the stars in the deep,
Grew stranger and stranger the more I brooded thereon!

OLAF. Am I not to myself a mysterious riddle?
Am I Olaf Liljekrans, the nobly born,
The knight so proud, who vaunted his race,
Who laughed the singing of birds to scorn!
And yet, from my heart I tear what I was!
Happy I am,—and that can I understand—
Your prophecy failed,—I should happiness find,
When the fairest of flowers I had found in the land.
Ah! happiness here I have found!

ALFHILD. I prophesied nothing.
But—tell me more of the life that is yonder!

OLAF. The life that is yonder may go its own way;
Here is my home; with you will I wander,
My lovely wife! Alfhild, behold!
Is it not as if here in the mountainous fold
Were built for us two a bower so fair!
The snowdrops in splendor stand garbed everywhere;
In here there is feasting, there is joy, there is mirth,
More real than any I have found on this earth!
The song rings out from the river so deep;
It is that which makes me both laugh and weep!
The song of magic, the mysterious lay,
Has made me so free, so happy and gay!

[Seizes her passionately in his arms.]

OLAF. Farewell to the village below I say!
'Tis here that my bridal-bed I shall prepare;
Farewell to the world forever and ay, —
For here I shall hold my beautiful bride!

ALFHILD. [Moves away apprehensively.] Olaf!

OLAF. [Stops suddenly, as if seized with a vague and painful
remembrance.] My bride! What is it I say!
Tell me — when first — I happened this way —
Can you still remember the very first night?
What was it I sought? — No longer I know!
Did I come to fetch you — to — the village below?
Did I come the wedding guests to invite?

ALFHILD. What mean you? Wedding? I can't understand — ?

OLAF. Our betrothal at Guldvik was held, you remember!
For three weeks thereafter our wedding was planned —
But it seems to me that, — no, my brow like an ember
Burns hot! I will try no more to remember!

CHORUS. [Softly and far in the forest.]
Olaf Liljekrans! Olaf Liljekrans!
Why sleep you so deep and so long?

ALFHILD. Hush, Olaf! do you hear?

OLAF. Did you hear it too?

ALFHILD. What was it?

OLAF. A memory of long ago,
Which often comes back when I wander with you!
'Tis evil, — it calls from the village below.

LADY KIRSTEN. [Aside, as she enters from the rear of the stage
unobserved by the others.] Ah, there! He speaks; could I understand — !

[Approaches listening.]

OLAF. [With increasing vehemence.]
Yes, yes, I come; not alone will I ride!
For ladies and knights shall heed my command,
And come hither with song to greet my bride!
For you shall be saddled my swiftest steed,
The poet and minstrel shall ride in the lead,
Thereafter shall follow the steward and priest,
The people shall all be bid to the feast!
Pages so courtly shall guide your steed,
And beautiful flowers be strewn at your feet,
The peasant shall bow to the ground like a weed,
His wife shall curtsy to you as is meet!
The church bell shall ring to the countryside:
Now rides Olaf Liljekrans home with his bride!

CHORUS OF WEDDING GUESTS. [Animated, yet softly, in the forest
to the left.]
  Now hasten we all
  To the wedding hall!
  The foal runneth light and gay!
  The hoofs resound
  On the grassy ground,
  As the merry swains gallop away!

LADY KIRSTEN. [Aside during the chorus.]
Heaven he praised then! Hemming has told — !

ALFHILD. [Jubilant.]
They come, they come, their voices I hear!
How sweetly it sounds! O Olaf, behold!

  LADY KIRSTEN. Olaf, my son!

  [Rushes to him unobserved by ALFHILD, who continues to look
out to the left.]

OLAF. God help me! What's here!
My mother!

LADY KIRSTEN. My poor unfortunate son!
Now are you saved from the evil one!
There comes Lord Arne with Ingeborg, your wife!

OLAF. [With a cry and as if suddenly awakening.]
Ingeborg! — With that have you shattered my life!
My happiness then was not what it seemed!
Alas, that you had to inform me of this!

OLAF. [In despair.]
Dear mother! a beautiful dream I have dreamed;
You waken me now, — there's an end to my bliss!

＊ ＊ ＊ ＊ ＊

SCENE XIII

[The Preceding. ARNE, INGEBORG, HEMMING, WEDDING
GUESTS, and LADY KIRSTEN from the left.]

ARNE. Good luck, Lady Kirsten, to you! You have found him
again, I am told.

LADY KIRSTEN. Of course I have found him. — And now for
home!

ARNE. [To OLAF.] And no harm has been done you?

OLAF. [Absent-minded.] Me! What do you mean?

LADY KIRSTEN. [Interrupting.] Of course not, Lord Arne! He
went astray on the hunt and —

INGEBORG. [Pointing to ALFHILD.] But this young woman — ?

LADY KIRSTEN. A poor child! She has given him lodging and shelter.

ARNE. But there is no one who lives up here.

LADY KIRSTEN. Yet a stray one here and there! There is many a solitary family still dwells among the mountains since the time of the plague.

ARNE. Then come, come! The horses are waiting below on the hill.

OLAF. [Painfully, as he glances at ALFHILD.] O mother! I cannot!

LADY KIRSTEN. [Softly and resolute.] You must! It will be your eternal shame if you —

ARNE. What does he mean?

LADY KIRSTEN. He is sick and tired as yet, but it will pass off. Come!

LADY KIRSTEN. [With a significant look at OLAF.] The young woman comes too!

INGEBORG. You mean that she — !

LADY KIRSTEN. Faithfully has she nursed him; it is only fitting that she be rewarded.

ARNE. And tomorrow the wedding is held!

LADY KIRSTEN. Tomorrow, — that I solemnly swear!

ARNE. I have your word!

HEMMING. [Softly and triumphant, as he brings forth the ring.] And I have Ingeborg's golden ring!

INGEBORG. [Takes the ring from him and says carelessly.] My ring! Aha, — so you have my ring, Hemming! Thanks, I shall now take care of it myself!

[HEMMING stands a moment dumfounded and then follows very slowly the rest, who all except ALFHILD go out to the left.]

* * * * *

SCENE XIV

[ALFHILD. Shortly afterwards THORGJERD from the back-ground.]

ALFHILD. (Has observed in silent and childlike amazement the preceding scene without however heeding the action; when they are gone she suddenly comes to herself as from a dream.)

They are gone! Can I trust my eyes; — is it true?
Yes, here in the moonlight they stood in full view!
There I see them again down the mountain side,
And I must go with them, for I am the bride!

[Starts as if to rush out to the left.]

THORGJERD. [In the background.]
Alfhild! my child! And how come you here?
I have told you before —

ALFHILD. O my father dear!
Now must I be free — as free as the wind,
No longer can I in the hills be confined!

THORGJERD. [Comes nearer.] What has befallen you?

ALFHILD. [In ecstasy.] Now is he come!

THORGJERD. But who?

ALFHILD. The fair knight! He will carry me home!
Now first do I grasp all the restless desire,
That long has been smouldering in me like fire!
We often have sat, as the river rushed by,
While you sang of the princess enthralled in the hill!
The princess, my father! the princess am I;
But he, the fair knight, bent the troll to his will! —
And now I am free to do what I may;
I will hence into life and its motley affray!
His words were like song! I am free as the wind;

No power can stay me or hold me behind!

THORGJERD. Poor child! You would down to the village below;
It will cost you your happiness; stay, do not go!

ALFHILD. But, father, I must! Your sweetest lays
Will seem to me now like a misty haze!

THORGJERD. Then go, my Alfhild! and dream while you may,
Your father will guard you alway!
But look you take care of the crafty young swains
With words so cunning and free!

ALFHILD. Away in the distant and sunny domains,—
Where Olaf is, there must I be!
There stands his castle with golden hall!
From the ballads you sang his face I recall;
The king's son is he, the knight who can ride,
And I, the poor Alfhild,—I am his bride!
Poor, did I say,—no, the princess on high,
O, more than the princess,—his sweetheart am I!

[The wedding chorus is heard far down the mountain side.]

ALFHILD. Listen, he calls with his trumpet and horn!
Farewell now, forest and flower and thorn!
Farewell, my valley; you have cramped me too long,
The whole world is calling with laughter and song!
Tomorrow attired in gold I shall ride
Away to the church as Olaf's bride!
We shall sit on the throne of honor within—
Ah, now shall my life in its fulness begin!

[She rushes out to the left. THORGJERD gazes after her thoughtfully. The chorus dies away in the distance as the curtain falls.]

* * * * *

SECOND ACT

[The enclosure on Lady Kirsten's estate. To the right is seen the main building with an opening in the gable; neither windows nor doors are visible. Further towards the back of the stage on the same side a small log church and a churchyard. On the left side a storehouse and other out-buildings. On both sides in the foreground simple benches of stone. It is afternoon.]

SCENE I

[LADY KIRSTEN. Servants and Maids occupied with preparations for the wedding.]

LADY KIRSTEN. Let there be no lack of food or drink.

LADY KIRSTEN. [To herself.] Hard have I labored and struggled to bring things to this point; but now I shall give a feast that shall be heralded far and wide.

LADY KIRSTEN. [To the servants.] Be sure to see that on the banquet table—yet no, I shall attend to that myself. The wine shall be poured into the silver flagons; the large drinking horns shall be filled with the Italian cider; the ale is for the servants only, and likewise the homebrewed mead;—and listen, be sure to see that there are enough yellow candles in the church; the bridal party are not to go to the altar until late in the evening, and with red lights shall they be escorted on their way from the banquet hall to the church. Go now, all of you, and see that you remember, every one of you, the things I have told you.

[The people go.]

LADY KIRSTEN. God knows this wedding is costing me more than I well can bear; but Ingeborg brings with her a good dowry and besides—Oh, well, Arne I shall no doubt be able to manage and rule as I see fit, if he is first—

[Looks out to the right.]

LADY KIRSTEN. There comes Olaf! If only I knew that he —

* * * * *

SCENE II

[LADY KIRSTEN. OLAF comes from the house in festive garb; he is pale and thoughtful.]

OLAF. [To himself.] Yesterday and today! There is but a midsummer night between the two, and yet it seems to me that both autumn and winter have overtaken my soul since the time I wandered up there on the mountain side — with her, with Alfhild!

OLAF. [Notices Lady Kirsten.] Alas, my dear mother, are you there?

LADY KIRSTEN. Quite so, my son! I like to see you dressed in gold and in silk. Now one can see by your dress who it is that is bridegroom tonight. I see you have rested.

OLAF. I have slept, but little have I rested; for all the while
I was dreaming.

LADY KIRSTEN. A bridegroom must dream, — that is an ancient custom.

OLAF. My fairest dream is ended; let us not think any longer about that.

LADY KIRSTEN. [Changing the subject.] We shall have a merry time today, I think.

OLAF. It does not appear that heaven is pleased with my wedding day.

LADY KIRSTEN. How so?

OLAF. There are indications of a storm. Do you see how heavily the clouds are gathering in the west?

LADY KIRSTEN. The brighter the festive candles will shine when you go to the church tonight.

OLAF. [Paces back and forth a few times; at length he stops before his mother and says.] If I had married a poor man's daughter, without family or wealth,—tell me, mother, what would you have done?

LADY KIRSTEN. [Looks at him sharply.] Why do you ask?

OLAF. Answer me first. What would you have done?

LADY KIRSTEN. Cursed you and gone to my grave in sorrow!— But tell me, why do you ask?

OLAF. Ah, it was only a jest; I little thought of doing so.

LADY KIRSTEN. That I can believe; for you have always held your family in high honor. But be merry and gay; tomorrow Ingeborg will sit in there as your wife, and then you will find both peace and happiness.

OLAF. Peace and happiness. One thing there is lacking.

LADY KIRSTEN. What do you mean?

OLAF. The fairest of flowers which I was to pick asunder and scatter far to the winds.

LADY KIRSTEN. The silly dream;—think no longer about it.

OLAF. Perhaps it would be best for me if I could forget.

LADY KIRSTEN. In the ladies' room your betrothed sits with all her maids; little have you talked with her today. Do you not want to go in?

OLAF. [In thought.] Yes, yes! Where is she?

LADY KIRSTEN. In the ladies' room, as I said.

OLAF. [Lively.] Nothing shall be lacking to her from this day. Shoes with silver buckles I shall give her; she shall wear brooches and rings. The withered twigs shall be put away; I shall give her a golden necklace to wear.

LADY KIRSTEN. Of whom do you speak?

OLAF. Of Alfhild!

LADY KIRSTEN. I was speaking of Ingeborg, your betrothed. Olaf! Olaf! You make me anxious and worried, — so strange are you. I could really almost believe that she had bewitched you.

OLAF. That she has! Yes, forsooth, mother, I have been bewitched. I have been in the elf maidens' play; happy and gay I was as long as it lasted, but now —. Through long, long years I shall be weighed down with woe as often as I call it to mind.

LADY KIRSTEN. If she were a witch, the stake would surely be hers; but she is a crafty and wily woman who has lured you on with her fair speech.

OLAF. She is pure as the mother of God herself!

LADY KIRSTEN. Yes, yes, but beware! Remember, whatever she is, tomorrow you are wed; it would be both sin and shame to you if you longer took notice of her.

OLAF. I realize it, mother, full well!

LADY KIRSTEN. And Ingeborg, whom you have betrothed and who loves you, yes, Olaf! loves you with all her heart — the punishment of heaven would be visited on you, in case you —

OLAF. True, true!

LADY KIRSTEN. I will not speak of our own circumstances; but you can easily see that Arne's daughter can help us greatly in one thing or another; our affairs have been going from bad to worse, and if the harvest should fail this year I should not in the least be surprised if we had to take up the beggar's staff.

OLAF. Yes, I know it.

LADY KIRSTEN. With Arne's money we can mend everything; an honorable place you will win for yourself among the king's men. Think this carefully over; if you have promised Alfhild more than you can fulfil — and I seem to notice in her something like that in spite of her quiet demeanor — why, speak with her about it. Tell her, — well, tell her anything you please; empty-handed she shall not go away from here, — that you can freely promise. See, here she comes! Olaf, my son! think of your betrothed and your noble race, think of your old mother who would have to go to her grave in shame, in case — be a man, Olaf! Now I go in to look after the banqueting table.

[Goes into the house.]

* * * * *

SCENE III

[OLAF alone.]

OLAF. [Gazes out to the right.]
As merry she is as the youthful roe,
As it plays with no thought of the morrow;
But soon will she wring her small hands in woe,
And suffer in anguish and sorrow!
Soon must I destroy the faith in her heart,
And waken her out of her dreams.
And then — yes, then we forever must part.
Poor Alfhild! So bitter your fate to me seems!

OLAF. [Brooding.]
What cared I for honor, what cared I for power,
What mattered my race when I wandered with you!
It seemed in your eyes was reflected a flower,
More precious than any the world ever knew!
Forgotten I had both struggle and strife,
But since I again came home to this life,
Since at table I sat in my father's hall,
Since I went to answer my mother's call —

OLAF. [Abruptly.] 'Tis true from a noble race I am born,
And Alfhild lives up in the mountains forlorn.
In her I should find but a constant sorrow.
I must tell her — yet, no, I can't let her know!
Yet truly — I must — I must ere the morrow,
She must hear what to me is the bitterest woe!

* * * * *

SCENE IV

[OLAF. ALFHILD from the church.]

ALFHILD. [Runs eagerly to meet him.]
Olaf! Olaf! You have led me to the land
Where I walk amid flowers, where before I trod on sand.
In truth you have here so pleasant an isle,
O here I can live without worry or guile!
So much I would question, so little I know,
The riddles must you explain as we go. —
Is it green here always in summer and spring?

OLAF. Alfhild!

ALFHILD. Your answer delay!
You see yon house with its spire and wing?
There went I this morning to play;
Without there was joy, there was laughter and mirth;
Within it was still as nowhere on earth.
I stepped through the door, I saw a great hall,
Within was a peace that was fair;
A dawn softly breaking pervaded it all,
And people were kneeling in prayer.
But high from above them a virgin looked down,
She sailed upon clouds of white,
Her head shone forth like a crimson crown,
Like heaven when dawns the light.
Calm was her face, a blue dress she wore,
A beautiful elf in her arms she bore,
And round about her played angels of love,
That laughed when they saw me below in the door
From their place in the heavens above!

OLAF. [Aside.] Alas! I have wrought so woeful a play,
Soon will her sorrow begin!

ALFHILD. O, tell me, Olaf! what people are they
Who live in the house I was in?

OLAF. Each one who like you is good and kind,
Each one who is child-like in spirit and mind.
'Tis the church, God's house, — it belongs to him.

ALFHILD. The mighty father! 'Tis only your whim!
His house is high over the stars in the sky,
Where the white swan sails undefiled,
So high 'tis beyond any mortal eye
Save that of the dreaming child! —
The church that you spoke of! So then it is there
We shall ride in festal procession,
As bridegroom and bride!

OLAF. [Aside.] No longer I dare
Delay my wretched confession!

ALFHILD. Ah, each of your words has burned like a coal,
And deep its mark it has left on my soul!
My bosom is filled with joy and with song;
Wherever I wander in field or at home,
They shine on my path, they light me along, —
Like stars at night in the heavenly dome!
You said the whole world would be asked to the feast,
And foremost should ride the minstrel and priest,
Knights should go forward and guide my steed,
And roses should blossom on every side,
Each lily we met should bow like a weed,
The flowers should curtsy before the bride!

OLAF. Have I said —

ALFHILD. Olaf, you surely recall!
All things have followed your every desire;
The lindens stand yonder so green and so tall;
The roses are decked in their festive attire
And dance like elves at an elfen ball.
Never did heaven's illumining eye
So radiantly shine as here from the sky;
Never before sang the birds so sweet!
They sing the bride and the bridegroom to greet! —
O, you — you make me so happy and blessed,
Both heaven and earth could I hold to my breast!
Nowhere can so humble a weed be found
Which under my feet I could crush and destroy,
Nowhere a creature so deep in the ground,
But I would share in its sorrow and joy!
My bosom is filled with the glory of spring;
It surges and roars like a wood in a storm!

OLAF. [Aside.] And soon this youthful and lovely form
Shall writhe beneath sorrow's tormenting sting!

ALFHILD. O, glorious life!

[She kneels with upstretched arms.]

ALFHILD. O father of love,
In the distant heaven! Had I but the power,
The tongues of the angels above,
Thy praise I should sing every hour;
I cannot, for I am of little worth,
I can only bow down before you to the earth —
O thanks, thou unspeakable! Glory and praise
For all I can here understand of thy ways!

[She rises.]

ALFHILD. Yes, lovely is life in its every breath,
As lovely almost as the journey to death!

OLAF. In the grave you think it is pleasant to lie?

ALFHILD. I know not your meaning, but I brooded long.
And asked of my father "What means it to die?"
In answer thereto he sang me a song:

"When the child of man is weighted with grief
And longs to be rocked to rest,
Then comes there an elf with wings of white
And frees its spirit oppressed.

"The little elf with his wings of white
Makes ready a downy bed,
Of lilies he weaves the linen sheets
And pillows of roses red.

"Away on the pillows he carries the child,
He carries it safe on his arm,
He takes it to heaven aloft on a cloud
Away from all earthly harm.

"And cherubs there are in the heaven above
(I tell what is true to you);
They strew the pillows of rosy red
With pearls of white and of blue.

"Then wakens the little earthly child,
It wakens to heavenly mirth, —
But all that happiness, all that joy
There's no one that knows here on earth."

OLAF. 'Twere better, alas! had you never come here,
Had you lived in the mountain your peaceful life.
Your joy like a weed will wither and sear,
Your faith will be killed —

ALFHILD. But as Olaf's wife
I am strong as the torrent and have no fear!
With you by my side let happen what may,
With you I will laugh and suffer and languish.

ALFHILD. [Listening.] Hush, Olaf! You hear that mournful lay,
It sounds like a song of the bitterest anguish!

CHORUS OF PALLBEARERS. [Softly outside to the right.]
  The little child we carry
  With sorrow to the grave,
  Beneath the mould we bury
  What soon the worms will crave.

  Hard is this lot and dreary:
  With mournful dirge and sigh
  To carry sad and weary
  The child where it shall lie!

ALFHILD. [Uncertain and anxious.]
What is it, Olaf? What is it, I say?

OLAF. A child that death is bearing away,
A mother and children weep on the way.

ALFHILD. Death! Then where are the pillows of red,
The lily-white linen, and where is the dead?

OLAF. I see no pillows of red or of gray,
But only the dark black boards of the bier;
And thereon the dead sleeps on shavings and hay.

  ALFHILD. On shavings and hay?

  OLAF. That is all there is here!

ALFHILD. And where is the elf who bears on his arm
The child far away from all earthly harm?

OLAF. I see but a mother whose heart will break,
And little children who follow the wake.

ALFHILD. And where are the pearls of blue and of white,
That the angels strew in the heaven of light?

OLAF. I see only this, — they weep many a tear
As they stand at the side of the bier.

ALFHILD. And where is the home, the house of God,
Where the dead dream only of mirth?

OLAF. Behold! Now they place him beneath the sod
And cover him over with earth.

ALFHILD. [Quiet and thoughtful, after a pause.]
Not so was death in the song — not so.

OLAF. 'Tis true; but no such joy and pleasure
Has any one felt here below. —
Have you never heard of the mountain king's treasure,
Which night after night like gold would glow;
But if you would seize the gold in your hand,
You nothing would find save gravel and sand;
And listen, Alfhild! it often is true
That life turns out in the selfsame way;
Approach not too near, it may happen to you,
That you burn your fingers some day.
'Tis true it may shine like a heavenly star,
But only when seen from afar.

[He becomes aware of Lady Kirsten off the stage to the right.]

OLAF. My mother—she'll tell you—I shall depart.
The angels above send their peace to your heart!

[He goes towards the house but is stopped by LADY KIRSTEN.—
The sky becomes overcast with dark clouds; the wind begins to
howl in the tree-tops.—ALFHILD stands absorbed in deep
thought.]

　　* * * * *

SCENE V

[The Preceding. LADY KIRSTEN.]

LADY KIRSTEN. [Softly.] Not so, my son, you have told her—?

OLAF. All I was able to say I have said. Now you tell her the rest,
and then, mother, let me never, never see her again.

[He casts a glance at ALFHILD and goes out past the house.]

LADY KIRSTEN. That folly will soon be burned out of his soul,
if—

LADY KIRSTEN. [As if she suddenly has an idea.] But in case I—
Ah, if that could succeed, then would he be cured,—that I can
promise. But Alfhild—? Well, nevertheless, it must be attempted.

ALFHILD. [To herself.]
　So then there is here too anguish and woe;
　Well, so let it be; I shall never despair.
　The sorrow of earth I never need know,
　Still Olaf is good and fair!

LADY KIRSTEN. [Approaches.] It seems to me that gloomy
thoughts are weighing upon your mind.

ALFHILD. Yes, yes, the result of things I have recently heard.

LADY KIRSTEN. From Olaf?

ALFHILD. Certainly from Olaf; he has told me—

LADY KIRSTEN. I know, Alfhild. I know what he has said.

LADY KIRSTEN. [Aside.] He has mentioned to her his wedding, I see.

LADY KIRSTEN. [Aloud.] This very night it is to be held.

ALFHILD. What is to be held?

LADY KIRSTEN. The wedding!

ALFHILD. [Eagerly.] Oh, yes, that I know!

LADY KIRSTEN. You know it and do not take it more to your heart than this?

ALFHILD. No. Why should I take it to heart?

LADY KIRSTEN. [Aside.] There is something she is meditating, — I see that clearly.

LADY KIRSTEN. [Aloud.] Well, so much the better for all of us. But tell me, when the wedding is over, what then will you do?

ALFHILD. I? I have little thought of that.

LADY KIRSTEN. I mean, have you in mind to remain here or to go home?

ALFHILD. [Looks at her, surprised.] I have in mind to remain!

LADY KIRSTEN. [Aside.] There we have it; she thinks to hold him in her wiles even after he is wed. Well, we shall see about that.

LADY KIRSTEN. [Aloud.] Alfhild! I wish you every possible good, and if you dared rely on my —

ALFHILD. Yes, that I certainly dare!

LADY KIRSTEN. Well and good; then you will let me take upon myself your happiness. I shall take charge of you as best I know how, and if you but give me your word you shall this very night go to the church as a bride.

ALFHILD. Yes, I know that.

LADY KIRSTEN. [Surprised.] You know that! Who has told you?

ALFHILD. Olaf himself said so.

LADY KIRSTEN. [Aside.] Has Olaf—? Yes, forsooth, he has had the same idea that I had, to marry her off in order to be rid of her. Or perhaps in order to—well, no matter,—when she is finally married, when Olaf on his side is a married man, then—

LADY KIRSTEN. [Aloud.] Well and good, Alfhild! If Olaf has told you our intention for you, then it is not necessary for me to—But do you now hasten, go in there in the store house; there you will find my own wedding gown; that you shall wear!

ALFHILD. [With childlike joy.] Shall I! Your own wedding gown!

LADY KIRSTEN. Do as I say. Go in there and dress yourself as splendidly as you please.

ALFHILD. And do I also get a bridal crown?

LADY KIRSTEN. Certainly! A bridal crown and silver rings and golden bracelet. You will find plenty of them in the coffers and chests.

ALFHILD. Silver rings and golden bracelets!

LADY KIRSTEN. Go, go, and hurry as fast as you can.

ALFHILD. O, I shall not be long about it.

[Claps her hands.]

ALFHILD. I shall have silver rings and golden bracelets!

[She runs out to the left.]

* * * * *

SCENE VI

[LADY KIRSTEN alone.]

LADY KIRSTEN. The evil and cursed woman! Happy and gay she is though she knows that Olaf is to wed another. But that very fact will serve me well; it will go easier than I had thought. She looks as innocent as a child, and yet she can agree to take him as a husband whom I first pick out for her. And I who thought that she truly loved Olaf! If he is still ignorant of her real spirit, he shall soon learn. He shall know her to the core, he shall know how she has bewitched and lured him, and then, well, then she is no longer dangerous.

LADY KIRSTEN. [Smiling.] Well, well! Olaf thought of the same way of saving himself that I did; so good-natured I had never imagined him. — But where shall we find the man who is willing to — well, she is pretty, and I shall not mind a little silver and even a bit of land. Has Olaf already spoken to some one? That is hardly thinkable! — Well, then I shall see to that. I have servants enough on the estate and —

[Looks out to the right.]

LADY KIRSTEN. Hemming! what if I should try him! But he saw them together in the mountain yesterday; he must surely know there is something between the two. But none the less — he is a humble serving-man, and poor besides, and weak of mind — we shall see, we shall see!

* * * * *

SCENE VII

[LADY KIRSTEN. HEMMING from the right.]

HEMMING. [To himself.] Nowhere is Ingeborg to be found; she will bring me to my grave, — that is certain. Yesterday she was gracious to me; she gave me her ring; but then she took it away from me again; and today she will not so much as look at me as I pass.

LADY KIRSTEN. [Slowly, as she approaches.] A little cautious I must be.

LADY KIRSTEN. [Aloud.] Ah, Hemming, is it you? You prefer to wander alone, I see; you keep yourself away from the servants and maids; when I see such things I realize very well that you do so not without reason.

HEMMING. Why, my noble lady! what should —

LADY KIRSTEN. Yes, Hemming! there is something that you keep all to yourself as you go about; you are not very cheerful!

HEMMING. [Disconcerted.] Not cheerful? I?

LADY KIRSTEN. [Smiling.] There is here today a young and beautiful girl whom you fancy very much.

HEMMING. All saints!

LADY KIRSTEN. And she in turn has a fancy for you.

HEMMING. Me — Whom? I do not know whom you mean.

LADY KIRSTEN. Come, Hemming, do not speak so; before me you need not feel ashamed. Yes, yes, I see clearly, I tell you.

HEMMING. [Aside.] Heaven! she must have noticed by Ingeborg's manner that —

LADY KIRSTEN. I have seen that the wedding is but little joy to you. The trip to the church you care little about, since you would yourself like to go as a groom, yet cannot see your way clear.

HEMMING. [In the greatest agitation.] Alas, Lady Kirsten! my noble, august lady! be not offended!

LADY KIRSTEN. [Surprised.] I? And why should I be offended?

HEMMING. [Continuing.] I have struggled and fought against this unhappy love as long as I have been able, and I honestly believe she has done the same.

LADY KIRSTEN. She? Has she then told you that she cares for you?

HEMMING. Yes, almost!

LADY KIRSTEN. Well and good; then you talked about it together?

HEMMING. Yes, — but only once, only one single time, I swear.

LADY KIRSTEN. Once or ten times, it is all the same to me.

LADY KIRSTEN. [Aside.] Then they are already agreed; it was certainly a stroke of luck that I came upon Hemming; now I am not at all surprised that Alfhild was so willing to go to the altar.

LADY KIRSTEN. [Aloud.] Hemming! I am much indebted to you for finding my son again and for otherwise being of help to me; now I shall make requital, — I shall to the limit of my power stand by you in the matter we just spoke of.

HEMMING. [Overcome with joy.] You! You will! Lady Kirsten! Alas, great God and holy saints! I hardly dare believe it.

LADY KIRSTEN. [Stops.] But Lord Olaf, your son! What do you think he will say?

LADY KIRSTEN. He will not interpose any objection, — I shall see to that.

HEMMING. [Unsuspecting.] Yes, truly, it would be best for him too, for I know she cares little for him.

LADY KIRSTEN. [Smiling.] That I have noticed, Hemming!

HEMMING. Have you! Well, you are so clever, Lady Kirsten! And I who thought that I was the only one who had noticed it.

HEMMING. [Doubtfully.] Do you think that Lord Arne will give his consent?

LADY KIRSTEN. Your master? I shall know how to talk him into it, — that will not be so difficult.

HEMMING. You think so? Alas, but I am so poor a man.

LADY KIRSTEN. I shall remedy that all right, in case Lord Arne is not prepared to do so.

HEMMING. Thanks, thanks, Lady Kirsten! Heaven reward you for your kindness!

LADY KIRSTEN. But you will keep this that we have been speaking of to yourself.

HEMMING. That I promise.

LADY KIRSTEN. Then hold yourself in readiness; the guests will assemble out here in a little while now, and do you be on hand.

[She goes over to the door of the store house and looks for ALFHILD.]

HEMMING. [To himself.] No, this is to me like a strange illusive dream. Ingeborg and I, — we are to belong to each other! Ah, can it be true? So high I never dared let my thoughts ascend; — it seemed to me in the morning that I had been guilty of the greatest presumption if during the night I had dreamed about it. — Hm! I know very well of course that it is not for my sake that Lady Kirsten goes to all this trouble. She has something up her sleeve; she thinks it necessary to break the agreement with Lord Arne, and now that she has noticed that Ingeborg cares for me she will use that as an excuse. Well, I have so often given my master warning, but he will never believe me.

ARNE. [Calls outside to the left.] Hemming! Hemming!

LADY KIRSTEN. [Comes forward.] Your master calls! Go now! After a while I shall speak to him; he will agree. Believe me, he shall follow his page to the church in the same hour that he leads his daughter thither.

HEMMING. Thanks, thanks, Lady Kirsten! Truly, you confer a blessing on us all.

[He goes out to the left.]

LADY KIRSTEN. [To herself.] So young she is and yet so cunning; she has been coquetting with Hemming all the while she made my son believe that — Well and good, he shall soon learn to know her arts. But first I must see Lord Arne; he thinks highly of Hemming and would reluctantly part with him; it seemed too that Hemming feared that something like that might stand in the way; but they can easily remain as they are even if Hemming marries. — Hemming sees more clearly in the affair than I had expected. What will Olaf say, he asked; he has evidently noticed that my son still thinks of Alfhild. Well, let him; if he takes her he will say nothing, and when Alfhild is married, — I know Olaf; he has always wanted to stand in high honor among the men of the village, and for that reason he will certainly — yes, yes, it must, it shall succeed.

[She goes out to the right.]

* * * * *

SCENE VIII

[HEMMING comes from the left with a bowl of ale hidden under his coat. ARNE follows him cautiously, looking about.]

ARNE. Is there anyone?

HEMMING. No, come along, master.

ARNE. But it seemed to me I heard Lady Kirsten.

HEMMING. She is gone now, come along!

ARNE. [Sits down on the bench to the left.] Hemming! it is well that the wedding is to be held tonight. Tomorrow I go home; yes, that I will. Not a day longer will I remain in Lady Kirsten's house.

HEMMING. Why, master! is there enmity again between you?

ARNE. Is it not enough, do you think, that she and all her superior relatives look down on me; at supper they laughed and jested among themselves because I could not bring myself to eat of all those ungodly, outlandish dishes. And what was it that we got to drink? Sweet wine and cider that will stay in my stomach for eight days. No, the good old homebrewed ale for me.

[Drinks and adds softly and bitterly.]

ARNE. Of this I had sent the wretched woman three full barrels. And what has she done? Thrown it to her servants, and here I must steal myself a drink, — yes, Hemming! steal myself a drink of my own ale, that they may not revile me as a coarse peasant, who doesn't understand the more refined drinks.

HEMMING. Well, master! I gave you warning.

ARNE. Ah — gave me warning! You are stupid, Hemming! You think
I haven't noticed it myself; but wait, just wait!

ARNE. [Flaring up.] To place my good nourishing ale before the house servants, as though it were not worthy to be put on the table of a lord. —

HEMMING. Yes, Lady Kirsten treats you ill, that is certain.

ARNE. [Hands him the bowl.] Come, sit down and drink!

ARNE. [HEMMING sits down.] Listen, Hemming! I could wish we were home again.

HEMMING. Well, I have no fancy for this festive home.

ARNE. No, my old room at Guldvik for me; — when we sat there of an evening and played chess with the ale jug between us —

HEMMING. The while Mistress Ingeborg sat at the loom and embroidered roses and all sorts of flowers in the linen —

ARNE. And sang all the time so merrily that it seemed to me that I became young and active again. Yes, Hemming! when the wedding is over, we shall go back and live our old ways again.

HEMMING. But then there will be no one who works the loom and sings merry lays the while.

ARNE. No, that is true enough; Ingeborg will then be gone. It will be a little hard on me; she is wild and self-willed, but I shall miss her nevertheless, — miss her greatly.

ARNE. [Considers.] Now and then I suppose I could visit her here — But no, that I will not! Here they laugh at me, they whisper behind my back, — I see it well enough.

HEMMING. But in case you wished, it could still be changed.

ARNE. Changed! You are stupid, Hemming! Always you talk about changing.

ARNE. [Hands him the bowl.] Come, drink, it will do you good. Changed; no, no, it shall never be changed! It was evil spirits who put into my head the idea of marrying into Lady Kirsten's family. But now it is done; the superior kinsmen will have to behave as they please, but my own relatives and friends shall not laugh at me, — if I have given my word, I shall keep it too.

ARNE. [Disheartened.] If I only knew that Olaf would be kind to her; I shall ask him to — .

ARNE. [Vehemently.] He *shall* be kind, else I shall come and beat him with my old fists.

HEMMING. Yes, it is well that you keep your eye on her, for Olaf cares little for her, I do believe.

ARNE. So, you think so?

HEMMING. Do you remember Alfhild, the poor girl, who yesterday followed us down from the mountain?

ARNE. Indeed I do. She is pretty!

HEMMING. [Rises.] So thinks Olaf, too.

ARNE. What does that mean?

HEMMING. Olaf loves her! 'Tis many a time he visited her up there; — what Lady Kirsten has told you, you must never believe.

ARNE. And what you blab about I believe still less. You are provoked with Ingeborg because at times she makes fun of you, and therefore you begrudge her this attractive marriage; yes, yes, I know you too well.

HEMMING. Why, master! you could believe that —

ARNE. Make me believe that Olaf Liljekrans loves that beggar woman! A noble, high-born lord such as he! It is almost as if one were to say that Ingeborg, my daughter, had a fancy for you.

HEMMING. [Embarrassed.] For me — how could you ever imagine —

ARNE. No, I don't imagine! But the one is as unreasonable as the other. Come, drink! and don't talk any more such nonsense.

ARNE. [Rises.] There is Lady Kirsten with the guests. What's going to happen now?

HEMMING. They are all to assemble out here; they will then follow the bride and bridegroom to the banquet-table and thence to the church.

ARNE. Aye, what a cursed custom! To the church at night! Is then marriage a work of darkness?

* * * * *

SCENE IX

[The Preceding. LADY KIRSTEN, OLAF, INGEBORG, GUESTS, and SERVANTS and MAIDS enter gradually from the several sides.]

LADY KIRSTEN. [To herself.] I have not seen Olaf alone; but when I think it over, it is probably best that he know nothing about it until it is all over.

LADY KIRSTEN. [Softly, to HEMMING, who has been whispering with INGEBORG.] Well, Hemming! How do you think your master is disposed?

HEMMING. Alas, Lady Kirsten! I have but little hope unless you lend your aid.

LADY KIRSTEN. Aye, we'll manage it all right.

[She mingles with the GUESTS.]

INGEBORG. [Softly, to HEMMING.] What do you mean? What blessed hope is it you are speaking of?

HEMMING. Alas, I hardly dare believe it myself; but Lady Kirsten means well by us. She will soon show you that —

INGEBORG. Hush! they are approaching.

OLAF. [In an undertone.] Tell me, mother! how goes it with her?

LADY KIRSTEN. Well enough, as I knew before.

OLAF. Then she knows how to comfort herself?

LADY KIRSTEN. [Smiling.] It seems so. Only wait! This very evening you shall know for certain.

OLAF. What do you mean?

LADY KIRSTEN. I mean that she is a sly witch. All her fair words have been deceitful wiles.

OLAF. No, no, mother!

LADY KIRSTEN. That we shall see! Alfhild is happy and gay, — so much I know.

OLAF. It were well for me if she were!

LADY KIRSTEN. [Loudly and clearly.] Lord Arne of Guldvik! Now is the hour come at length which we have all, I imagine, been looking forward to.

HEMMING. [Aside.] Now it begins!

LADY KIRSTEN. Soon will the church bestow its blessing on our children and unite them in a long and loving union.

HEMMING. [Aside, startled.] What now?

LADY KIRSTEN. The terms we have already agreed upon. But I suggest that we here once again seal them with hand and word.

HEMMING. [As before.] Heaven and earth! Is she trying to deceive me?

ARNE. That is not necessary; I stand by my word like an honorable man.

LADY KIRSTEN. That I well know, Lord Arne! but it will take but a moment. First of all, there shall be an end for all time to every quarrel and dispute between our families, — and as for the damages and injuries which our old disagreements have caused on either side, no one shall demand compensation for them; each must manage them as best he knows how. We promise that, do we not?

ARNE. That we promise!

[General shaking of hands among the relatives of the bridal couple.]

HEMMING. [Softly.] Curses upon you; you lied to me shamefully!

LADY KIRSTEN. Then we mention again, what we are already agreed upon, that the boundary line between Lord Arne's domains and mine shall be moved as far in upon his land as good and impartial men may judge to be fitting and just.

ARNE. Yes, yes, I suppose it must be so!

LADY KIRSTEN. That we promise, then?

THE GUESTS. That we promise!

[Shaking of hands as before.]

LADY KIRSTEN. Finally, Lord Arne shall give in the form of a dowry to his daughter as much silver, linen, and other furnishings as were named and agreed upon at the betrothal feast, all of which shall here be placed in my home from the day Mistress Ingeborg moves herein as my son's lawful wife, which is tonight. On that we are agreed?

THE GUESTS. That we solemnly promise!

[Shaking of hands.]

LADY KIRSTEN. Then let the bride and bridegroom clasp hands and go to the banquet-table and thence to the church.

ARNE. [Aside.] Ah, Hemming can now see whether Lady Kirsten deceives me.

HEMMING. [Softly.] O, then it is all over for me; a fool I was to depend on her.

LADY KIRSTEN. But on this joyful day it is fitting that we make as many as possible happy. And therefore I have a request to make, Lord Arne!

ARNE. Speak forth! If I can I shall gladly comply.

HEMMING. [Aside.] What does she purpose now?

LADY KIRSTEN. There is still a young couple who would like to go to the altar this evening; from what I hear, they are agreed between themselves. The bride I shall take care of, but the bridegroom you must assist; it is Hemming, your page, and Alfhild!

INGEBORG. [With a cry.] Hemming!

OLAF. [Likewise.] Alfhild!

HEMMING. O, woe is me! Now I understand —

THE GUESTS. [At the same time.] Hemming and Alfhild! The mountain girl!

[Laughter and whispering.]

OLAF. Alfhild! You will marry her off to—No, no, it shall not be! Never, never!

LADY KIRSTEN. Be still!—Olaf, my son; be still, I beg you!

ARNE. [To himself.] What's this! Yes, truly, then Hemming was right; there is something between Olaf and Alfhild.

ARNE. [Whispering.] Aye, Lady Kirsten! I see your scheme. Now I know why Olaf wandered three days in the mountain, and now you intend to make use of Hemming to be rid of her. Ha, ha!

LADY KIRSTEN. [With forced composure.] Lord Arne! how can you believe such a thing?

ARNE. [In a low tone.] O, I see clearly! Now I should think I had very good reason to break the agreement.

LADY KIRSTEN. [Softly and frightened.] Break the agreement! I beg of you! Will you put us all to shame?

[They talk together softly.]

HEMMING. [To INGEBORG, with whom he has in the meantime been whispering.] That is all there is to it, I swear. Lady Kirsten and I have not understood each other.

INGEBORG. Well, then decline! You shall! I command you.

HEMMING. No, no! I dare not; she will then see that it was you I was thinking of.

INGEBORG. Good; then I shall.

INGEBORG. [Aloud.] Hemming shall not go to the altar with Alfhild;—he is too good to marry another man's darling!

OLAF. [With a cry.] For shame!

THE GUESTS. Darling!

ARNE. [To INGEBORG.] What are you saying?

LADY KIRSTEN. Heaven protect us!

OLAF. Cursed be my soul! She is put to shame!

INGEBORG. Yes, loudly I proclaim it: she is another man's darling. Let him gainsay it who dares.

ARNE. Ingeborg!

ARNE. [Aside.] What is the matter with her?

LADY KIRSTEN. [Softly.] So that's the way it is! She then, — she it is who cares for Hemming!

LADY KIRSTEN. [Softly and clearly, to ARNE.] Do you now intend to break the agreement? You can now see for yourself from your daughter's conduct what reason I had to get Hemming married!

ARNE. [Disconcerted.] My daughter! Could you imagine that she —

LADY KIRSTEN. You need not pretend! Ingeborg has a fancy for your house-carl; now I should think I had good reason to break our agreement.

ARNE. Break, break —! What are you thinking of! To bring on me such disgrace!

LADY KIRSTEN. [Mocking.] Yes, — otherwise you would do it!

ARNE. [Quickly.] No, no, I have reconsidered; it is best we both keep still!

LADY KIRSTEN. [To herself.] See, now have I won! I know Olaf; a woman so scorned will never tempt him!

* * * * *

SCENE X

[The Preceding. ALFHILD comes unnoticed out of the storehouse in glittering bridal dress with a crown on her head and her hair flowing.]

210

ARNE. [Aside.] This has been a cursed day for me! O, he is a cunning dog, this Hemming! He knew that Ingeborg had a fancy for him; it was therefore so galling to him that Olaf should have her.

LADY KIRSTEN. [Who has in the meantime regained her composure.] And now to the festive hall! Hemming we can think of later. — Olaf, take your bride by the hand!

ARNE. [Reluctantly, as he sees INGEBORG whisper to HEMMING.]
Where is the bride? Come, come!

ALFHILD AND INGEBORG. [At the same time, as they each seize one of OLAF's hands.] Here I am!

THE GUESTS. How, — she takes Olaf?

[General amazement.]

LADY KIRSTEN. [Aside.] So far has he gone, then!

LADY KIRSTEN. [Aloud, to ALFHILD.] You are mistaken! That is not your bridegroom!

ALFHILD. Why, certainly, it is Olaf!

INGEBORG. [Lets go his hand.] If then he has promised her — !

LADY KIRSTEN. [In great agitation.] Olaf is not your bridegroom, I say! Tell her it yourself, my son!

[OLAF is silent. LADY KIRSTEN's Kinsmen look at each other embarrassed. ARNE's Relatives draw nearer, angry and threatening.]

LADY KIRSTEN. [With raised voice.] Olaf Liljekrans! Answer loudly and clearly! You owe it to yourself and to us.

OLAF. [In despair, struggling with himself.] Let it be as you wish then, mother! Yes, by all the saints! I shall answer. Alfhild! you are mistaken! I am not your bridegroom.

OLAF. [Pointing to INGEBORG.] There — there stands my bride!

ALFHILD. [Withdraws a step or two dumfounded and stares at him.]

She — your —

OLAF. [With rising irritation.] Alfhild! go hence! Go, go, far into
the mountain again; 'twill be best for you. I was sick and bewildered
in mind when I wandered up there! What I have told you I little
remember! I do not know and I do not want to know! Do you
hear, — I do not want to! — The golden crown you can keep! Keep all,
both the silver and gold, that you there stand dressed in. More, —
yea, tenfold more you shall have. — Well! why do you stare at me
so?

[ALFHILD takes off the crown and the other adornments and
places them at OLAF's feet as she continues uninterruptedly to stare
at him.]

OLAF. Perhaps I pretended to you that you were to be my bride
tonight, perhaps you believed me! Perhaps you thought that Olaf
Liljekrans would marry a — a — what was it you called her?

OLAF. [Stamps with his foot.] Do not stare at me so, I say! I know
you well enough; you have bewitched me. I forgot my family; I
forgot my bride, my betrothed, she who stands there.

OLAF. [Seizes ALFHILD violently by the arm.] Look at her,
Alfhild! Aha, it is she that I love!

[ALFHILD sinks down on her knees and covers her face with her
hands.]

OLAF. Rise, Alfhild! rise, I say! If you dare to grieve in this way, I
shall kill you! — Why are you not happy? Be merry and wild as I
am! — And the rest of you! Why do you stand so silently, looking at
one another? Laugh, — laugh loudly, so that it may echo around! —
Alfhild! Why don't you answer? Have I not told you enough! Aha!
Then add, you others, a word to what I have said! Come, say something, you too; Lady Kirsten would like it! Laugh at her, mock her,
trample her under your feet!

OLAF. [With ringing laughter.] Ha, ha, ha! She is Olaf's darling!

[ALFHILD sinks down to the ground in such a way that she rests
prostrate against the stone bench at the left. A flash of lightning

illuminates the scene and the thunder rolls; during the following to the close of the act the darkness and the storm increase.]

OLAF. See, see! That I like; now do the powers above join in! Right now will I ride to the church with my bride! Come, Mistress Ingeborg! But first will we drink,—yes, drink, drink! Bring here the beaker and horn,—not in there—! Light the candles in the church! Let the organ resound; prepare for a dance—not mournful psalms—fie, fie, no, a dance!

[Thunder and lightning.]

OLAF. Ah, it is rumored in heaven that Olaf Liljekrans is celebrating his wedding!

[Rushes out to the right.]

ARNE. Christ save me! his reason is gone!

LADY KIRSTEN. Ah, have no fear; it will soon pass,—I know him.

[Draws ARNE aside with her.]

ARNE. [Gently threatening HEMMING in passing.] O, Hemming, Hemming! You are a sly dog!

[The GUESTS go quietly and gloomily out to the right; the SERVANTS to the left.]

INGEBORG. [Detains HEMMING.] Hemming! I will not go to church with Olaf Liljekrans!

HEMMING. Alas, what will prevent it?

INGEBORG. If it comes to that, I shall say no,—no before the very altar itself, in the presence of all!

HEMMING. Ingeborg!

INGEBORG. Hold my horse saddled and ready!

HEMMING. What! You will—!

INGEBORG. I will! Now I know for the first time how dear you are to me, — now when I stand in danger of losing you. Go, — do as I say, and let me know when it is time.

[She goes out to the right.]

HEMMING. Yes, now am I strong; now I dare venture whatever it be!

[He goes out to the left.]

* * * * *

SCENE XI

[ALFHILD. Later HEMMING, INGEBORG, and others at various times.]

ALFHILD. [Remains lying motionless for a long time with her face concealed in her hands. At length she half raises herself, looks about bewildered, rises, and speaks with quiet broken laughter.]
One falcon the heavens with plenty may bless,
Another must suffer great want and distress!
One bird wears a coat of feathers so gay,
Another must live contented with gray!
I have known that tears are a balm to the soul,
When the world is nothing but gall;
But now I have suffered such sorrow and dole,
I could laugh myself dead at the thought of it all!

[It is now quite dark. The windows of the church are being lighted up. ALFHILD goes over to the house and listens while the following song is heard faintly within.]

CHORUS OF WEDDING GUESTS.
Hail to the bridegroom and hail to the bride!
There's feasting and joy everywhere.
Lord Olaf, all hail! a knight who can ride,
And Ingeborg a lady so fair!

HEMMING. [Steals in from the left during the song.] The horse stands saddled and ready! Now a secret sign to Ingeborg and then away!

[He goes out to the right to the rear of the house.]

ALFHILD. His health from the silvery cup they drink,
The bride sits proudly enthroned at his side;
The candles of wax on the altar now wink,
Soon out to the church they will ride!
Within at the banquet sit host and guest
And laugh as they bandy the merry jest!
But here I must wander alone in the night,
Alas, they have all forsaken me quite!
Olaf! The storm is rending my hair!
The rain beats against me wherever I fare!
Olaf, Olaf! Can you see me thus languish
Beneath this unspeakable torture and anguish?

[She laughs.]

ALFHILD. But rain or storm is a trifling thing,
'Tis as nothing beside the poignant sting
I suffer within my breast. —
My home and my father and all the rest
I left for Olaf, the friend I loved best!
He swore to me then I should be his bride!
And I came — God's love I felt in my soul;
But he drove me away, he thrust me aside;
So loudly he laughed when I writhed in dole!
While they banquet within, like a dog I must stay
Out here in the storm. Hence, — hence I will go!

[Starts to go, but stops.]

ALFHILD. But I have not the power, I cannot go away;
Here must I stay and suffer my woe!
'Tis little the flowers out there in the wood
Can tear themselves up from the ground!
And Olaf, whether he be false or good, —

About him my roots I have wound.

[Pause. — The HOUSE SERVANTS come with torches from the left.]

ALFHILD. [As if seized by an uneasy presentiment.] Whither do you go? Whither, whither? What is going to happen?

A SERVANT. Why, see, see! It is Alfhild; she is still here!

ALFHILD. O, tell me this! What is going to happen, — why all these preparations?

THE SERVANT. The wedding! Wouldn't you care to see it?

ALFHILD. [In feverish anxiety.] The wedding! O, no, no! Put it off, only till tomorrow! If the wedding is held, then is everything over with me, I well know!

THE SERVANT. Postpone it! No, Alfhild! 'Tis not, I'm afraid, the wish of bridegroom or bride!

ANOTHER. Think for a moment! Were you yourself but the bride, you surely would not want to wait.

[Laughter.]

THE FIRST SERVANT. Now we go down to the gate at the church to light the way with red bridal lights when the procession starts from the house.

THE SECOND SERVANT. Come along with us, Alfhild! You shall also have a torch to carry!

SEVERAL. Yes, yes, you must come! It is Lord Olaf's day of glory!

[Laughter.]

ALFHILD. [Takes one of the torches.] Yes, yes, I will! As the most humble in the row I shall stand down there, and then, when he sees me, when I ask of him, when I remind him of everything he has promised and sworn, — O, tell me, tell me, do you not think that he will be kind to me again? Do you think so? O, tell me you do! Say that you think so!

THE SERVANTS. Aha, — for certain he will; now come!

[They go out to the right to the rear of the house.]

ALFHILD. [Bursts into tears.]
They mock at me, laugh at me, — one and all!
So harsh is not even the mountain wall;
The moss thereon is permitted to grow;
There's no one so kind to me here! I — I must go!

[Thunder and lightning.]

ALFHILD. Ah, heaven itself is angry and grim,
It pours out its wrath on my wretched head;
But flash there is none to annihilate him
Who craftily tricked me in all that he said!

[The tones of the organ are heard from within the church.]

ALFHILD. O, listen! I hear God's angel choir!
'Tis Olaf to the altar they call!
And I must stand here in my ragged attire
And suffer outside the church-hall!

[She swings the torch high in the air.]

ALFHILD. No, no, that I will not, thou all-highest God!
O, tempt me no longer, forswear thee I may!

[She is silent and listens to the organ music.]

ALFHILD. God's angels are singing! From under the sod
The dead they were able to carol away!
O, my bosom is bursting with woe!

[She kneels and faces the church.]

ALFHILD. Cease, cease your melodies tender and sweet!
O, cease your singing; be kind, I entreat!
Or Olaf to the altar will go!

[Whispering and in the greatest apprehension.]

ALFHILD. Be still! O, be still! For a little while yet!
He is lulled in a sleep that will make him forget!
O, waken him not, else straight he will hie
To the church—and then, alas, I must die!

[The organ grows louder through the storm. ALFHILD springs up, beside herself with despair.]

The angels of God have forsaken me quite!
They mock at my anguish and woe!
They conjure him forth;—he is now in their might!
Ah, if here in the dark, dark night I must go,
Your bridal chamber at least shall be light!

[She throws the torch in through the opening in the gable and falls down on the ground.—INGEBORG and HEMMING come hurriedly from behind the house.]

HEMMING. Now it is time. The horse stands saddled behind the store house.

INGEBORG. And all the servants are down at the church, are they not?

HEMMING. Aye, rest you assured; and in the banquet house I have barred every shutter and door with heavy iron rings; no one can get out!

INGEBORG. Away, then! Up to the valley which Alfhild has told of!

HEMMING. Yes, up there! There no one will seek us!

[They rush out to the left.—ALFHILD continues to lie motionless for some time. Suddenly cries and commotion are hear in the bridal house; the flames break out through the roof.]

ALFHILD. [Jumps up in despair.]
It burns!—Aha,—I remember! 'T was here
Too dark for my soul—it filled me with fear!
Olaf, before it was you who smiled,

Now it is Alfhild, so gay and so wild! —
In the bridal house there is anguish and gloom,
The bride is burning on the arm of the groom!

[The HOUSE SERVANTS rush in one by one without torches and stand as if turned to stone. OLAF comes into view up in the opening, which he seeks to widen with desperate efforts.]

OLAF. Alfhild! 'Tis you! So might I have known!
If only from out of this danger you save me,
'T is silver and gold you shall hereafter own!

ALFHILD. [With wild laughter.]
Too well I remember the promise you gave me!
Now ride to the church with minstrel and priest!
Now hold your wedding, — forget all the rest!
Alfhild has honored you as she knew best, —
The torch she has swung at your bridal feast!

[She rushes out at the back. The SERVANTS hasten to lend their help; a part of the roof falls in; OLAF is seen high amidst the flames as the curtain falls.]

* * * * *

THIRD ACT

[A sunny valley, rich in flowers, trees, and vegetation of all kinds, and surrounded by lofty snow-capped mountains. In the center of the background a quiet mountain tarn; on the left side a rocky cliff which drops straight down to the water. On the same side nearer the front of the stage a very old log hut, almost entirely hidden in the dense shrubbery. The glow of dawn shines over the mountains; in the valley itself the day is only half begun; during the following scene's the sun rises.]

SCENE I

[ALFHILD lies sleeping and half concealed among the bushes beside the hut; soft music indicates her shifting dreams. OLAF comes down the hillside to the right. Over his wedding clothes he wears a coarse cloak.]

OLAF. Here it was; I know the green there this side of the tarn. It was yonder beneath the linden tree that I dreamed my strange dream. On the slope of the mountain there I stood when Alfhild for the first time came to meet me; I placed my betrothal ring on the string of my bow and shot;—that shot has proved a magic shot; it struck the huntsman himself.

OLAF. It is strange that when I wander up here, far from the village below, it seems as if another atmosphere played around me, as if a more vigorous blood flowed in my veins, as if I had another mind, another soul.

OLAF. Where is she now?

OLAF. I shall,—I will find her again! Up here she must come; she has no home out there in the cold wide world. And I—am I not also a homeless fugitive? Did I not become a stranger in my mother's house, a stranger among my kinsmen, the very first hour I met her?

OLAF. Is she then a witch, — has she power over secret arts as — ?

OLAF. My mother! Hm! It seems to me it would scarcely be well for me to allow her to manage my life; she insinuates thoughts into my heart which do not belong there. No, no, I will find Alfhild again and ask forgiveness for the wrong I have done, and then —

[He stops and looks out to the left.]

* * * * *

SCENE II

OLAF. (Alfhild still sleeping. Thorgjerd comes from behind the hut on the left.)

OLAF. Well met, stranger!

THORGJERD. Thanks, the same to you. You are early about!

OLAF. Or late; early in the morning, but late in the night.

THORGJERD. You belong in the village below, I take it.

OLAF. My family lives there. And you?

THORGJERD. Wherever the mind is at rest, there is one at home; that is why I like best to wander in here; — my neighbors shall not do me any injustice.

OLAF. That I have noticed.

THORGJERD. Then you have been here before?

OLAF. I chased a hind this summer in here; but when I look closely I see 'tis a royal child that has been bewitched.

THORGJERD. [Looks at him sharply.] That hunt is dangerous!

OLAF. For the hunter?

[THORGJERD nods.]

OLAF. I was sitting and thinking the same thing myself; it seems to me that I was bewitched on that hunt.

THORGJERD. Farewell and good luck to you!

OLAF. Out upon you! If you wish a huntsman good luck he will never come within shot of the prey.

THORGJERD. If the shot should strike the hunter himself, the best luck that could happen to him would be to have no luck at all.

OLAF. You speak wisely.

THORGJERD. Yes, yes; there is many a thing to be learned in here.

OLAF. Too true! I have learned here the best that I know.

THORGJERD. Farewell! I'll take greetings from you to your kinsmen.

OLAF. You mean to go down?

THORGJERD. Such was my purpose. These are merry days down there, I am told. A mighty knight is celebrating his wedding —

OLAF. Then you should have been there last night; now I fear the best part of the fun is past.

THORGJERD. I dare say I'll come in time even yet.

OLAF. Perhaps! But still you should have been there last night; so bright and so warm a festive hall you never have seen before.

THORGJERD. It was well for him who was within.

OLAF. I know one who had to stand outside.

THORGJERD. Yes, yes, outside, — that is the poor man's place.

OLAF. I know one who had to stand outside and who nevertheless was both worse off and better off than those within.

THORGJERD. I must go down, — I see that clearly; I shall play for the guests. Now I shall fetch my harp, and then —

OLAF. You are a minstrel?

THORGJERD. And not among the worst. Now shall I fetch my harp from where it lies hidden near the waterfall; those strings you should hear. With them I sat once on the edge of the bed and played the bride out of the festive hall over ridge and field. — Have you never heard little Ingrid's lay? He who could play the bride out of the bridegroom's arms can surely play his child home to her father again. Farewell! If you linger here we may meet again when I get down there.

[He goes out to the right by the tarn.]

* * * * *

SCENE III

[OLAF. ALFHILD.]

OLAF. Ah, if it were—for certain I cannot doubt it. Alfhild herself said that her father played such music that no one who heard it could ever forget. He mentioned Lady Ingrid who disappeared on the eve of her wedding many years ago,—there was a young minstrel named Thorgjerd who loved her, so went the story. Many a strange tale was afterwards current about him; at times he stood right in the midst of the village and played so beautifully that all who heard it had to weep; but no one knew where he made his home. Alfhild—yes, she is his child! Here she has grown up, here in this desolate valley, which no one has known of by name for many a year; and Ingrid, who disappeared—indeed, he said—

[Becomes aware of ALFHILD.]

OLAF. Alfhild! There she is! In her wedding garments she has fled up here. Here then shall you awaken after the bridal night; so sorry a day to you was my day of honor. You wished to go out into life, you said; you wanted to learn to know all the love in the world. So sorry a journey you had, but I swear it shall all be well again. She moves; it is as if she were writhing in sorrow and anguish;—when you awaken, it shall be to joy and delight!

ALFHILD. [Still half in dreams.]
It burns! Oh, save him,—he is within!
He must not die! Life anew he must win!

[She jumps up in fright; the music ceases.]

ALFHILD. Where am I! He stands here before me, it seems!

Olaf Liljekrans! save me from my dreams!

OLAF. Alfhild! take heart, here you need fear no harm!

ALFHILD. [Moves away, fearfully and apprehensively.]
You think with sweet words my soul to beguile?
In your heart there is evil, though with lips you may smile,
On me you shall nevermore practice your charm!

OLAF. Alfhild! be calm, do not start;
'Tis Olaf I am, the friend of your heart!
Unkind I have been, I have treated you ill;
But deep in my heart I was faithful to you!
I was blind and deluded and weak of will, —
And thus I did wound you far more than I knew!
O, can you forgive me? Alfhild, you must, —
I swear to you I shall be worthy your trust!
I shall bear you aloft and smooth your way,
And kiss from your cheek the tears of dole,
The grief in your heart I shall try to allay,
And heal the wound that burns in your soul!

ALFHILD. I know you too well and your cunning disguise.
Since last I did see you I too have grown wise.
You would have me believe with your wily speech
It is you for whom I now suffer and languish.
You would have me believe it was you that did teach
Me to revel in joy and to writhe in anguish.
'Twill profit you little, I know you too well,
Whether early or late you come to my dell.
I know you too well; for deceit on your brow
I can read. Not so was the other, I vow!

   OLAF. The other? Whom mean you?

ALFHILD. He that is dead!
'Tis therefore I suffer so bitter a dread.
You don't understand? You must know there were two;
And that is why peace I shall nevermore find!
The one was all love, so good and so true,
The other was evil, faithless, unkind;
The one to me came on a late summer day,

When my heart burst in flower and bloom;
The other led me in the mountain astray,
Where all things are shrouded in gloom!
'Tis the evil one, you, that has come again;
The other who loved me, so good and so kind,
The one who will never be out of my mind, —
Ah, him have I slain!

[She sinks down on a stone near the house and busts into tears.]

OLAF. Has he stolen your peace, has he robbed you of rest,
Then why let him longer dwell there in your breast!

ALFHILD. Alas, were I laid in the grave far below,
With me, I am sure, my sorrow would go!
I knew it not then, — to you do I swear,
I thought it was little for him I did care;
Now I see I must die of a grief-broken heart,
Yet his image will never depart!

[A short pause.]

ALFHILD. Have you chords in your bosom that you can command?
It seems so; your voice sounds so pleasant and sweet;
Pleasant — though blended it is with deceit.
Have you chords in your breast, then go round in the land
And sing of Alfhild a plaintive lay
To the village girls you meet on the way:

Only yesterday I was so little a roe,
I roamed in the green groves around;
They came to the forest with arrow and bow,
And chased me with falcon and hound!

Only yesterday I was a bird so forlorn,
I sat 'neath the linden alone;
They drove me away from the place I was born,

And threw at me stone after stone.

Only yesterday I was an untamed dove,
Which nowhere finds peace or rest;
They came from below, they came from above,
And pierced with an arrow my breast!

OLAF. [Deeply moved.]
  Alas, that I lay in the grave below.
  Lulled in eternal rest!
  Your every word is a steel-made bow
  That strikes with an arrow my breast!

ALFHILD. [Jumps up with childlike joy.]
Just so it shall be, — 'tis rightfully so!
Yes, truly, indeed, have you chords in your breast!
So let it be sung; they easily show
That you are yourself by my sorrow oppressed.
They show that your own grief is just as strong
As the one that you voice in your plaintive song!

  [She stops and looks sorrowfully at him.]

ALFHILD. Yet no, — you shall not sing of Alfhild's lament;
What stranger is there whom my sorrow will move!
From whence I came, and whither I went
There is no one out there who shall question or prove!
Sing rather of Olaf Liljekrans,
Who wandered astray in the elf-maidens' dance!
Sing of Alfhild, the false and unkind,
Who drove his betrothed quite out of his mind;
And sing of all the sorrow and fear,
When dead Olaf Liljekrans lay on the bier.
Sing of all the weeping below,
When away they carried the three who had died!
The one was Olaf, the other his bride!

The third was his mother who perished of woe.

OLAF. Yes, Olaf is dead; it is just as you say;
But I shall be now so faithful a friend;
Wherever you dwell, wherever you wend,
From your side I shall nevermore stray!
May I suffer in full for the sin I committed, —
Atonement to me shall be sweet.
'Twill comfort me much if I be permitted
To roam with you here in some far-off retreat!
From early dawn till the end of day,
Like a faithful hound I shall follow your lead!
I shall clothe my remorse in so plaintive a lay
Till finally you shall believe me indeed.
Each moment we spent here in ecstasy
I shall call up again to your memory!
Each flower that blooms shall speak it anew,
The cuckoo and swallow shall sing it to you!
The trees that grow here in the forest so green
Shall whisper thereof both soft and serene!

ALFHILD. Enough! You would only beguile me anew;
Far better were it for you now to depart!
So fair is the falsehood I see within you,
So faithless the thoughts that dwell in your heart!
What would you up here? What is it you want?
You think that you know the place that you haunt?
So pleasant a spot was this valley of yore,
A curse lies upon it forevermore!
In the past, when lone in the forest I went,
The leaves on the trees had so fragrant a scent!
The flowers bloomed forth on my every side,
When you pressed me to you and called me your bride!
But now — the whole valley is burned in the night;
The trees are burned to the left and the right;
The straw and the leaves are withered away,
Each flower is turned to a dusty gray! —

ALFHILD. Yes, clearly I see, — in a single night
Is the world become old! — When I wandered below
All alone, and sank down 'neath my shame and my woe,
Then faded the world and its golden delight.
All things but deceit have vanished away;
So much have I learned on my bridal day!
My father lied; he was wrong when he said
The dead are borne to the dwelling of God;
But Olaf knew better the fate of the dead:
The dead sink below, far under the sod!

ALFHILD. [She breaks out in deepest agony.]
Ah, well do I see now you knew what you did;
For low in the grave my body is hid.

OLAF. Alfhild! Your words deal so crushing a blow!
O, God! was your heart once so young and so bold —
Forgive me my sin and forget all your woe!

ALFHILD. [With marked and increasing bewilderment.]
Hush, do not speak to me! Olaf, behold!
A corpse they carry, to the grave they creep;
But no mother is there, no children who weep,
No pillows are there of blue or of red, —
Alfhild on shavings and straw lies dead!
I shall never ride now to the heaven above,
And awake in the arms of the God of love.
No mother have I whose heart will break,
No one who follows and weeps for my sake;
No person have I in the world so wide,
Who weeps for me at the bier, —
No angels to scatter on every side
Blue pearls in the heavenly sphere;
And ne'er shall I reach the dwelling of God,
Where the dead dream only of mirth!

OLAF. Alfhild!

ALFHILD. They lower me under the sod!
They cover me over with earth!
And here must I lie with all my dread,
Must live and suffer although I be dead:
Must know there is nothing now left for me,
Yet cannot forget, nor fight myself free;
Must hear when he whom my love I gave
Rides off to the church right over my grave;
Must hear him forever suffer and languish,
And yet can not lessen his anguish!
O, how my bosom is filled with despair!
The angels of God have forgotten my prayer!
They heed no longer my weeping and woe —
The portal is closed to the heavenly bliss —
Dig me up again! Let me not lie here below!

[She rushes out to the left.]

OLAF. Alfhild! Alfhild! O, Christ, what is this?

[He follows her quickly.]

* * * * *

SCENE IV

[INGEBORG and HEMMING enter, after a pause, from the right.]

INGEBORG. Well, here we are up here! How lovely and bright and peaceful it is!

HEMMING. Yes, here we shall live happily together!

INGEBORG. But mark you well that you are my servant, and nothing else, — until my father has given his consent.

HEMMING. That he will never do!

INGEBORG. Never you mind, — we'll find some means or other. — But now we must think about choosing a cabin to live in.

HEMMING. There are plenty of them around here. Over the whole valley there are deserted huts; everything is just the same as it was when the last people died in the terrible plague many years ago.

INGEBORG. Here I like it very much! Over there, too, there is just such an old hut; the water is near by, and the forest must surely be alive with game. You can fish and hunt; aye, we shall live a wonderful life!

HEMMING. Yea, forsooth, a wonderful life! I shall fish and hunt the while you gather berries and keep the house in order.

INGEBORG. Do I? No, that you must take care of!

HEMMING. Yes, yes, as you please. O, a delightful life we shall live!

[Stops and adds somewhat dejectedly.]

HEMMING. But when I stop to think a bit; — I have neither bow nor fishing outfit.

INGEBORG. [Likewise with an expression of despondency.] And it occurs to me there are no servants here who can help me.

HEMMING. That shall I willingly do!

INGEBORG. No, thanks. — And all my good clothes — I didn't bring anything along except my bridal gown which I am wearing.

HEMMING. That was thoughtless of you!

INGEBORG. True enough, Hemming! And for that reason you shall steal down to Guldvik some night and bring me clothes and other things as much as I have need of.

HEMMING. And be hanged as a thief!

INGEBORG. No, you shall be careful and cautious, — that I warn you. But when finally the long winter comes? There are no people up here, — music and dancing we shall never have — Hemming! Shall we stay here or —

HEMMING. Well, where else is there we can go?

INGEBORG. [Impatiently.] Yes, but human beings cannot live here!

HEMMING. Why, surely, they can!

INGEBORG. Well, you see yourself they are all of them dead! Hemming! I think it best I go home to my father.

HEMMING. But what will become of me?

INGEBORG. You shall go to war!

HEMMING. To war! And be killed!

INGEBORG. Not at all! You shall perform some illustrious deed, and then will you be made a knight, and then will my father no longer be opposed to you.

HEMMING. Yes, but what if they kill me in the meantime?

INGEBORG. Well, we'll have plenty of time to think about that. Today and tomorrow we shall have to remain here, I suppose; so long will the guests sit in the festive house and celebrate, — if they look for us, it will probably be about in the village; up here we can be safe and —

[She stops and listens.]

CHORUS. [Far away off the stage to the right.]
  Away, — away to find
  Alfhild, the false, unkind;
  For all our woe and strife
  She must pay with her life!

HEMMING. Ingeborg! Ingeborg! They are after us!

INGEBORG. Where shall we find refuge?

HEMMING. Well, how can I know —

INGEBORG. Go into the hut; lock the door so that it can be bolted from within.

HEMMING. Yes, but —

INGEBORG. Do as I say! I shall go up on the hill the meanwhile and see if they are far away.

[She goes out to the right.]

HEMMING. Yes, yes! Alas, if only they don't get us!

[He goes into the house.]

* * * * *

SCENE V

[OLAF comes from the forest to the left. Immediately afterwards INGEBORG from the right.]

OLAF. [Looks about and calls softly.] Alfhild! Alfhild! She is nowhere to be seen! Like a bird she disappeared from my view into the wood and I—

INGEBORG. They are right close and —

[Stops, frightened.]

INGEBORG. Olaf Liljekrans!

OLAF. Ingeborg!

HEMMING. [Sticks his head out of the door and spies OLAF.]
Lord Olaf! So! Now is it surely all up with me!

[Withdraws hastily.]

INGEBORG. [Aside.] He must have ridden in advance of the rest.

OLAF. [Aside.] She must have come up here with her father to look for me.

INGEBORG. [Aside.] But I will not go with him!

OLAF. [Aside.] I will not stir from here!

INGEBORG. [Aloud, as she draws nearer.] Olaf Liljekrans! Now you have me; but you will do ill if you try to compel me.

OLAF. That is furthest from my mind!

INGEBORG. Why then come you here in company with my kinsmen?

OLAF. Do I? On the contrary, it is you who—

INGEBORG. That invention won't fool me; only a moment ago I saw the whole crowd —

OLAF. Who? Who?

INGEBORG. My father and our relatives!

OLAF. Up here?

INGEBORG. Why, yes, right close at hand!

OLAF. Ah, then is my mother with them.

INGEBORG. Of course, she is with them. But how can that frighten you?

OLAF. You see, — it is I they seek!

INGEBORG. No, it is I!

OLAF. [Astonished.] You!

INGEBORG. [Begins to grasp the connection.] Or — wait a moment — Ha, ha, ha! What an idea! Come, shall we two be honest with each other?

OLAF. Yes, that is exactly what I had in mind!

INGEBORG. Well, then, tell me, at what hour came you up here?

OLAF. During the night!

INGEBORG. I, too!

OLAF. You!

INGEBORG. Yes, yes! And you went away without any one's knowing it?

OLAF. Yes!

INGEBORG. I, too!

OLAF. But tell me —

INGEBORG. Hush, we have only a moment or two! And you fled up here because you had but little desire to go to the altar with me?

OLAF. Aye, how can you think —

INGEBORG. Yes, that I can easily think. Answer me now; we were to speak honestly.

OLAF. Well, then, it was therefore that I—

INGEBORG. Well and good, I did likewise!

OLAF. You, Ingeborg!

INGEBORG. And now you would rather not have any one come upon your tracks?

OLAF. Well, it can't be denied!

INGEBORG. I, too! Aha,—'tis a jolly coincidence; I fled from you, and you from me! We both fled up here, and now just as our relatives are after us we meet again! Listen, Olaf Liljekrans! Say we promise not to betray one another!

OLAF. I promise.

INGEBORG. But now we must part!

OLAF. I understand!

INGEBORG. For, if they found us together, then—

OLAF. Yes, then it would be still more difficult for you to be rid of me!

INGEBORG. Farewell! If ever I come to have a wedding you shall be my bride's man.

OLAF. And if anything like that should happen to me, you will, I am sure, accommodate me in the same way.

INGEBORG. Of course! Farewell! Farewell! And do not think unkindly of me.

OLAF. Indeed not; I shall give you my hand wherever we meet!

INGEBORG. I, too! Wherever we meet—only not at the altar.

[She goes into the house. OLAF goes into the forest on the right at the back.]

* * * * *

SCENE VI

[LADY KIRSTEN, ARNE of Guldvik, WEDDING GUESTS, PEASANTS and SERVANTS from the right.]

LADY KIRSTEN. See, here will we begin the hunt. Our people must spread about and search all around the tarn; — she shall come forth and then — woe upon her! no mercy or pity is there in my soul.

ARNE. What will you do then?

LADY KIRSTEN. Hold judgment upon her — right on the spot where she is found! All the damage she has done on my dominions I have power and authority to punish in accordance with reason and justice.

ARNE. Yes, but what good is that? What is lost can not thereby be won back again.

LADY KIRSTEN. No, but I shall get revenge, and that is no little gain. Revenge, — revenge I must have, if I am to bear and live down my loss and all the shame she has brought upon me. The storm last night ruined the whole of my year's crop; not a single uninjured straw is left in my fields; and in here, where she herself has said she has her home, here everything thrives and blossoms more luxuri-antly than I have ever seen! Is not that the operation of secret arts? Olaf she has snared so securely in her devilish net that he fled out of the village in the wildest storm to follow her. My house she burned clear to the ground; all the openings and doors she barred on the outside; — it was a miracle of God that the servants brought their timely help!

ARNE. Alas, alas; I am afraid if has cost two lives that I thought much of, — Ingeborg and my man Hemming!

LADY KIRSTEN. Come, come, Lord Arne! You must not com-pletely despair of them yet. Ingeborg may have escaped after all; the rest of us came out of it untouched in spite of the cunning of the cursed witch; — Ingeborg has been bewildered with fright and has sought refuge somewhere.

ARNE. Yes, yes, that may be the case with Ingeborg; but Hem-ming is past all hope, — of that I am sure!

LADY KIRSTEN. How so?

ARNE. O, he had become such a sly and contriving devil of late! He has let himself be shut in and burnt merely to get revenge over me; he knows I can't get along for a single day without him. O, I know him!

LADY KIRSTEN. Well, however it is, Alfhild we must capture; she shall be tried, condemned, and punished; I have misdeeds a plenty to charge her with.

ARNE. And I can mention a few in case it is necessary; she has stolen my dapple-gray horse from the stable; this morning it was gone with saddle and bridle.

LADY KIRSTEN. [Aside.] Ingeborg and Hemming gone, and his horse likewise; were I in his place I should know what to think.

LADY KIRSTEN. [Aloud.] Now let us divide and go about in small groups; he who first gets his eye on Alfhild shall blow the trumpet or horn; let the rest listen and follow the sound till we are assembled again.

[They go out at different sides.]

ARNE. [Who alone has remained.] And I, who am not acquainted here, — how am I to find my way.

ARNE. [Calls.] Hemming! Hemming!

[Stops.]

ARNE. I forgot, — he is —

ARNE. [Shaking his head.] Hm! It was a shameful trick he played.

[He goes out to the right.]

* * * * *

SCENE VII

[ALFHILD appears near the tarn to the left; she carries a little bundle.]

ALFHILD. I have wailed, I have wept, till my heart is sore;
I am weary and tired, I can weep no more!

[Sinks down on a stone in the foreground.]

ALFHILD. First to my father farewell I shall say!
Then into the mountains I make my way!
Down here I see Olaf wherever I go;
I must up in the heights to steel my mind!
I must deaden my grief, forget what I know,
And leave all the memories dear behind!

ALFHILD. The life in my dream had so rosy a hue!
'Tis nothing but fiction, nothing is true, —
'Tis nothing but nonsense and shifting lies;
Naught can be seized and held in the hand.
Naught must be looked at with open eyes,
Nothing stands proof when we understand!

[The sound of trumpets is heard from the wood.]

ALFHILD. My mother's heirlooms I take with me;
I shall bury them deep in the ground!
I shall bury them deep 'neath the tall birch tree,
Over yonder where Olaf I found!

[She opens her bundle and takes out a bridal crown and other ornaments.]

ALFHILD. This crown did my mother once wear on her head;
She too by the world then was tricked and misled,
She too then in love and its power believed.
Was she too so rudely deceived?
Was it only in jest that my father did sing

The pleasures that gladden the human breast?
Ah, then he should never have said anything;
His songs have robbed me of earthly rest;
His songs built a home for the ecstasies
Of life in my heart, — now in ruin it lies!

[The trumpets are heard again.]

ALFHILD. Silver indeed is a metal of worth,
'Twill never crumble like autumn hay.
Were it hid for a thousand years in the earth,
It would still glitter bright, it would never decay!
The pleasures of life are like autumn hay,
And sorrow like silver that glitters alway!

[Ties the ornaments together in the bundle.]

ALFHILD. A magic treasure I often recall,
From which dropped nine glorious pearls every night;
But no matter how many the pearls it let fall,
The treasure remained just as big and as bright!

ALFHILD. A treasure of magic, this sorrow of mine,
And from it shall drip by night and by day,
Not nine, — but ten thousand pearls that shine, —
Yet the treasure shall never decay! —
Yes, the world has made me so wise, — so wise!
Once I followed the clouds in their flight,
Flew dreaming with them on their path in the skies,
And called them the swans of the light!
I thought that the trees spread their branches so wide,
That I might walk in the shade;
I thought there was life in the mountain side.
A sorry mistake I have made.
Now I know better; — for man alone
Can revel in joy, can suffer despair.
In tree and in flower, friend there is none, —

My sorrow alone I must bear.

[She rises.]

ALFHILD. Away then! Up midst the ice and the snow, —
The grave is the only shelter below!

[She starts to leave.]

* * * * *

SCENE VIII

[ALFHILD, LADY KIRSTEN, ARNE, WEDDING GUESTS, PEASANTS and SERVANTS from various sides. Later OLAF LILJEKRANS.]

LADY KIRSTEN. There she is! Stand still, Alfhild! Do not try to escape, — else we shall shoot you.

ALFHILD. What do you want of me?

LADY KIRSTEN. That you shall learn soon enough.

LADY KIRSTEN. [Points to her bundle.] What is this you are carrying?

ALFHILD. My mother's treasures!

LADY KIRSTEN. Give it here! See, see! A crown of silver! Indeed, Alfhild! If you are your mother's only daughter I am very much afraid the bridal crown will nevermore be needed in her family.

LADY KIRSTEN. [To the Servants.] Bind her! She stands there and pretends to be sad; no one can know what she is scheming.

[ALFHILD is bound.]

LADY KIRSTEN. [Aloud and with suppressed passion.] The court is ready. As you all know, I have a legal and prescriptive right to protect my dominions, to pass judgment in accordance with the law of the realm on every one who does me harm on my own lands. This is what you, Alfhild, have presumed to do, and it is therefore that you now stand here accused before your judge. Defend yourself if you can, but do not forget it is a matter of life and death.

ARNE. But listen, Lady Kirsten!

LADY KIRSTEN. Excuse me, Lord Arne! I am within my rights here, and I intend to insist on them.

LADY KIRSTEN. [To ALFHILD.] Come forward and answer me!

ALFHILD. Do you but question me, — I shall answer!

LADY KIRSTEN. Many and grievous are the charges that are directed against you. First and foremost I charge you here with having beguiled my son, Olaf Liljekrans, with your unholy arts, so that he turned heart and soul away from his betrothed to whom he was pledged, — so that he, sick in heart, never at any time found peace in his home, but came up here to this unknown valley where you have had your home. All this could not have happened in any ordinary way; you are therefore accused of witchcraft, — defend yourself if you can.

ALFHILD. I have little to say in answer to this. Witchcraft you call that strange power that drew Olaf up here. Perhaps you are right; but this witchcraft was not of evil; — every hour that Olaf has been here God must surely have witnessed! Each thought that I have had of Olaf the angels of God must have known! And they had no occasion to blush.

LADY KIRSTEN. Enough, enough! You would add blasphemy to your transgression! Woe upon you, Alfhild! Your every word only adds weight to the scales. Yet, that is your affair!

LADY KIRSTEN. [To the rest.] I crave you all as witnesses to her answer.

[Turns to ALFHILD.]

LADY KIRSTEN. I charge you next with having again, this very night, with the aid of these same secret powers, met Olaf up here, and furthermore that you keep him concealed in here!

ALFHILD. There you are right! Secretly is he hidden here!

LADY KIRSTEN. You admit it?

ALFHILD. Yes, but however powerful you are, you will never be able to set him free. Perhaps it would be best for me if you were able; but neither you nor the whole wide world have the power to set him free!

LADY KIRSTEN. [In a violent outburst.] Now death will certainly be your punishment! Out with it, — where have you got him?

ALFHILD. [Presses her hands to her bosom.] In here—in my heart! If you can tear him out from it you can practice witchcraft better than I!

LADY KIRSTEN. That answer is nothing. Out with it, — where is he?

ALFHILD. I have answered!

LADY KIRSTEN. [With repressed irritation.] Good!

ARNE. [To the spectators.] Were Hemming alive he would have been able to get the truth out of her; he had become so crafty of late.

LADY KIRSTEN. Now the third charge against you: last night you set fire to my house and burned it clear to the ground. Perhaps human life has been lost, — that we not know as yet, — but whether or no, it will neither harm nor help your cause; for your intention to burn all of us is as clear as day. Do you deny my charge that you set fire to my home last night?

ALFHILD. I do not deny it; I have destroyed your house!

LADY KIRSTEN. And how will you extenuate your action?

LADY KIRSTEN. [With bitter mockery.] You shall not be able to say that you acted over hastily. Good opportunity you had, so far as I can remember, to stop and consider; you stood outside there, no one came near you, no one prevented you from deliberating as calmly as you could. Nor shall you say that the merriment of the festive occasion went to your head, nor that the wine distracted you; for you were not on the inside at all; you stood on the outside, and it was cool enough there, — the biting wind should have made you sober.

ALFHILD. Yes, I destroyed your house last night; but you and Olaf and all the rest of you out there have done me a greater wrong.

242

The world was to me a festive hall which belonged to the Great Father. The blue heaven was its roof, the stars were the lamps that shone from its ceiling. I wandered happy and rich in all this; but you, you threw a brand right in the midst of this golden splendor; now is everything withered and dead!

LADY KIRSTEN. Such talk will profit you little! Still once more I ask, where is Olaf Liljekrans, my son?

ALFHILD. I have answered!

LADY KIRSTEN. Then you have also passed your own sentence, and I shall confirm it.

[OLAF appears on the rocky cliff among the trees, unnoticed by the rest.]

OLAF. [Aside.] Alfhild! God help me! What is that?

[Withdraws unseen.]

LADY KIRSTEN. You have, in accordance with the law of the land, incurred the penalty of death as guilty of witchcraft and arson. This sentence is herewith pronounced upon you, and forthwith right here on the spot it shall be executed.

ARNE. But listen, Lady Kirsten!

LADY KIRSTEN. Judgment is pronounced! Alfhild shall die!

ALFHILD. Do as you please; little shall I be of hindrance to you. When Olaf denied his love, then ceased my life, — I live no longer.

LADY KIRSTEN. Take her up on the rocky ledge over there.

[Two Servants take ALFHILD up.]

LADY KIRSTEN. For the last time, Alfhild! Give me back my son!

ALFHILD. I will answer no more!

LADY KIRSTEN. Just as you please!

LADY KIRSTEN. [To the Servants.] Cast her down! No, wait! I have an idea!

LADY KIRSTEN. [To ALFHILD.] As you stand there, I remember you again as you yesterday came forward with the golden crown and thought you were worthy to be Olaf Liljekrans' bride. Now we soon shall see how much you are worth; there are present here peasants and servants and many humble men; — perhaps your life can still be saved! Yes, Alfhild! You stare at me, but so it is; I will be merciful to you!

LADY KIRSTEN (Turns to the rest.) You all know the old custom, that when a woman is sentenced to death for a capital offence, as she is, her life will be saved and she will be free if an irreproachable man comes forth and upholds her innocence and declares himself ready and willing to marry her. That custom you know?

ALL. Yes, yes!

ALFHILD. [Bursting into tears.] O, to be mocked, — mocked so terribly in my last hour!

LADY KIRSTEN. Well then, Alfhild! This custom you shall have the benefit of. If the most humble man in my company comes forth and declares himself willing to marry you, then are you free.

LADY KIRSTEN. [Looks about.] Is there no one who applies?

[All are silent.]

LADY KIRSTEN. Give her the silver crown; that shall go in the bargain; perhaps, Alfhild, you will then rise in value!

[The crown is placed on ALFHILD's head.]

LADY KIRSTEN. For the second time I ask, — is any one willing to save her?

[She looks about. All are silent.]

LADY KIRSTEN. Now for it; I am afraid your moments are numbered. Hear me well, you servants up there! Should no one answer my third call, then do you watch for a sign from me and cast her into the lake! Use now your arts, Alfhild! See if you can conjure yourself free from death.

LADY KIRSTEN. [With a loud voice.] For the last time! There stands the witch and incendiary! Who will save and marry her?

[She looks about. All are silent. — LADY KIRSTEN raises her hand quickly as a signal, the Servants seize ALFHILD; in the same moment OLAF rushes out on the ledge in full wedding garb.]

OLAF. I will save and marry her!

[He thrusts the SERVANTS aside and unbinds her. ALFHILD sinks with a cry on his bosom; he puts his left arm around her and raises his right arm threateningly in the air.]

ALL. [Stand as if turned to stone.] Olaf Liljekrans!

LADY KIRSTEN. Olaf Liljekrans, my son! What have you done? Disgraced yourself for all time!

OLAF. No, I blot out the shame and disgrace which I brought on myself by my treatment of her! My sin I shall expiate and make myself happy the while!

OLAF. [Brings ALFHILD forward.] Yes, before all of you I solemnly proclaim this young woman my bride! She is innocent of all that has been charged against her; I only have transgressed.

[Kneels before her.]

OLAF. And at your feet I beg you to forget and forgive —

ALFHILD. [Raises him.] Ah, Olaf! You have given me back all the glory of the world!

LADY KIRSTEN. You will marry her! Well and good; then am I no longer a mother to you!

OLAF. You will cause me great sorrow, although it is now long since that you were a real mother to me. You used me merely to build aloft your own pride, and I was weak and acquiesced. But now have I won power and will; now I stand firmly on my own feet and lay the foundation of my own happiness!

LADY KIRSTEN. But do you stop to consider —

OLAF. Nothing will I now consider, — I know what I want. Now first I understand my strange dream. It was prophesied of me that I was to find the fairest of flowers, — that I was to tear it asunder and strew it to all the winds. O, thus it has happened! A woman's heart is the fairest flower in the world; all its rich and golden leaves I have torn asunder and scattered to the winds. But be of good cheer, my Alfhild! Many a seed has gone too, and sorrow has ripened it, and from it shall grow a rich life for us here in the valley; for here shall we live and be happy!

ALFHILD. O, now I am happy as in the first hour we met.

LADY KIRSTEN. [Aside.] Ingeborg is gone; this rich valley belongs to Alfhild, — no one else has a claim to it —

LADY KIRSTEN. [Aloud.] Well, Olaf! I shall not stand in the way of your happiness. If you think you will find it in this way, then — well, then you have my consent!

OLAF. Thanks, mother, thanks! Now I lack nothing more!

ALFHILD. [To LADY KIRSTEN.] And me you forgive all my sin?

LADY KIRSTEN. Yes, yes! Perhaps I too was wrong, — let us not say any more of that!

ARNE. But I, then? And my daughter, whom Olaf had pledged — Yet, it is true, perhaps she is no longer alive!

OLAF. Of course she's alive!

ARNE. She lives! Where is she? Where?

OLAF. That I can not say; but I may say that we both in all friendliness have broken our pledge.

LADY KIRSTEN. You see, Lord Arne! that I —

ARNE. Well, my daughter shall not be forced upon any one. Alfhild was fated to marry a knight; the same may happen to Ingeborg.

ARNE. [With dignity.] Noble lords and honorable men, hear me! It has come to my ear that many of you hold me to be little skilled in courtly manners and customs. I will show you now you are completely mistaken. In the old chronicles it is frequently told that when a noble king loses his daughter he promises her hand and half his kingdom to him who may find her; he who finds Ingeborg shall receive her hand in marriage and in addition half of all that I own and possess. Are you with me on that?

THE YOUNG MEN. Yes, yes!

* * * * *

SCENE IX

[The Preceding. INGEBORG comes hurriedly out of the hut and pulls HEMMING behind her.]

INGEBORG. Here I am! Hemming has found me!

ALL. [ASTONISHED] Ingeborg and Hemming! Up here!

ARNE. [Irritated.] Ah, then shall—

INGEBORG. [Throws herself about his neck.] O father, father!
It will not avail you; you have given your word!

ARNE. But that did not apply to him! Now I see it all right; he has taken you away himself.

INGEBORG. No, to the contrary, father! It was I who took him away!

ARNE. [Frightened.] Will you be silent with such words! Are you out of your head?

INGEBORG. [Softly.] Then say "yes" right here on the spot!
Otherwise I shall proclaim to all people that it was I who—

ARNE. Hush, hush! I am saying "yes"!

[Steps between them and looks sternly at HEMMING.]

ARNE. It was you then who stole my dapple-gray horse with saddle and bridle?

HEMMING. Alas, Lord Arne!—

ARNE. O Hemming! Hemming! You are a—

[Stops to consider.]

ARNE. Well, you are my daughter's betrothed; let it all be forgotten.

HEMMING AND INGEBORG. O, thanks, thanks!

* * * * *

SCENE X

[The Preceding. THORGJERD with a harp in his hand has during the foregoing mingled with the people.]

THORGJERD. Aye, see, see! A multitude of people in the valley today!

THE PEASANTS. Thorgjerd, the fiddler!

ALFHILD. [Throws herself in his arms.] My father!

ALL. Her father!

OLAF. Yes, yes, old man! There are people and merriment in here today, and hereafter it shall always be thus. It is your daughter's wedding we are celebrating; for love has she chosen her betrothed, of love have you sung for her, — you will not stand in our way!

THORGJERD. May all good spirits guard you well!

ALFHILD. And you will remain with us!

THORGJERD. No, no, Alfhild!
A minstrel has never a place to rest,
His soul fares afar, he forever must roam!
For he who has music deep down in his breast,
Is never in mountains or lowlands at home;
In the meadows green, in the sheltering bower,
He must touch the strings and sing every hour,
He must watch for the life that lives in the shower,
Beneath the wild fjord, in the rushing stream,
Must watch for the life that beats in the soul,
And clothe in music what people but dream,

And give voice to its sorrow and dole!

OLAF. But sometime you will surely visit us here!
Now shall 'mid the birches a hall be erected;
Here, my Alfhild! shall you be protected.
I and my love will always be near,
No more shall your eye be dimmed with a tear!

ALFHILD. Yes, now I see, — life is precious and kind!
Rich as the fairest dream of the mind!
So dreary and black is never our sorrow, —
'Tis followed sometime by a bright sunny morrow!

ALFHILD. [Kneels.] O angels of God! you have led me aright,
Again you have granted me solace and bliss!
You guided my wandering past the abyss,
You steadied my foot that was weak and slight!
O, if with my mind I cannot understand, —
With my heart I'll believe to the last!
Yes, heavenly powers! You still watch o'er the land!
Clear is the sun when the dark storm is passed; —
From death and destruction my love did you save:
So now then let happen what may!
For now I am cheerful, now am I brave,
Ready for life and its motley affray!

ALFHILD. [With a glance at OLAF.] And when we at length —

[She pauses and stretches her arms above her head.]

ALFHILD. by the angels of love
Are borne to our home in the heavens above!

[The rest have formed a group around her; the curtain falls.]

0 1341 1463960 9

CPSIA information can be obtained at www.ICGtesting.com
Printed in the USA
LVOW101232210613

339670LV00001B/28/P

9 783842 429406